MY DEMONS

LOSING THE DEMONS SERIES: BOOK 1

BLYTHE KYNDAHL

DEDICATION

Thank you to all the indie authors to see that dreams can come true as long as you take a chance.

PROLOGUE

LEXI

2009

All my life I have been dependable and boring. I turned my homework in on time, if not early. I had the best grades in school, but turned down graduating valedictorian wanted to graduate a year early and go to college ahead of schedule. I have always wanted to get out of this town and away from people who thought money and power defines them. My parents worked hard for what they had and that is what they taught me to do. Yes, I was left home alone quite a bit, but my parents needed to work, and sometimes a social event was work. I couldn't wait to get to college; I could reinvent myself and hopefully find the guy of my dreams. Well, I guess I would settle for a guy who would follow in my dreams of starting a party planning business. I plan on traveling the world and will do it with or without a man by my side. I know it is a tall order, but with hard work and determination it will be a reality. It will be my reality.

I have always been one of the guys? I wish I understood

men better, that way I would know when something was amiss and try to fix it before it blew up. I have had a handful of boyfriends in my four years that I have been able to date. Well, I thought they were my boyfriends but nope, they would only look at me as a friend. Brad came along while I was still in high school. I thought things were different with him. He was my first love. He was my first everything. This relationship, like with everyone else, was short lived. I quickly learned that love doesn't determine the length of one's relationship, especially if those feelings are one-sided. . Like everyone else, it was short lived. When any another girl who would show interest in them came along, it would be over. I can't help but feel as I'm being settled for, and that thought makes me feel empty.

I met Justin during freshman orientation week. I thought things were going to change for me. In the beginning things were great. Justin showed interest in me and treated with kindness and respect. Not only did he shower me with affectionate texts and phone calls, but we went out every weekend and he helped me study for my exams. I remember one night when some of his female classmates made a snide remark, questioning why he was even with me. He told them to mind their own damn business, and then he whispered in my ear that I was beautiful. This was a pleasant change from my high school relationships. I finally felt hopeful that I'd have the life I always dreamed of.

I have no idea what happened, but something snapped in our relationship. Once again, I found myself being thrust back into my own personal hell.

CHAPTER ONE

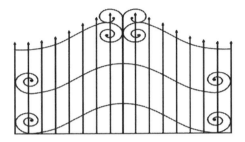

ROYCE

JBR is the most profitable breeding ranch in the United States. Anyone who wants to breed their animals whether; it is horses, bulls, dogs, we do it all. Our animals have won the many prestigious awards such as the Triple Crown, and Westminster Kennel Club best in show, just to name a couple. JBR, also known as The James Brothers Ranch, has been in my family since the early 1900's. As far back as I can remember my family has always made good choices and treated people with respect, and in return everyone treated them with respect. My brother and I were taught to always be polite and to live by the golden rule. For the most part living by such a guideline had paid off ten-fold. That was until the day the Kramer family discovered the JBR.

Everyone, whether you had money or not knew the Kramer family and about their business dealings. Law enforcement never could pin anything on them but, many of the buildings they own have more than one purpose.

It is rumored the family is involved in money laundering with a side gig of offering prostitution. That is the reason the Kramer name holds such power. They can ruin a person with a snap of their fingers or a flick of the wrist. One of the local businesses Justin and his family owned was the local bar. They were running prostitution out of it. On the outside of the building it looked like your local bar. Once you stepped inside their was a hallway that lead to the right and once you walked through the door at the end of the hallway you had entered a strip club, but in this strip club the men were aloud to touch the girls and do with them as they pleased. TO get into the door you had to have your name on the list. I couldn't not just walked in there. You had to be invited. One day the FBI was contacted by an onomous tip and the bar was shut down.

When the Kramers wanted a pure breed puppy, they came to JBR. The Kramer's were not satisfied with the puppy and took my parents to court. Of course my parents lost. My parents didn't want to take it that far, but the Kramers insisted. The ranch lost its dog breeding license. It was only an eighth of the total income the ranch brought in. Thankfully it wasn't that big of a hit. The Kramer's were displeased with the court ruling, but it was enough they never came back to the James land.

CHAPTER TWO

LEXI

Four Years Later

After a long day of classes, I stand in the doorway of my apartment watching my now ex-boyfriend Justin stroll out of my life.

"How could you Justin?" I shout standing by the door. My heart is crumbling to the ground. I found out after being together for three and a half years, the person I had built my life around has been cheating on me the whole time. He's been sleeping with the girls on the female debate team. I found a DVD sitting on my desk with a love note, of all things, from Justin. It's been a long time since Justin left me a note. I was curious. I was hopeful that maybe he realized what a jerk he was being. Maybe things would get better, I told myself. I was wrong. Popping the video into the DVD player, my stomach felt sick. Apparently one of these girls had been recording their rendezvous and thought it'd be a good idea to show me. My skin crawled at the images I saw. The passion he had for these women that he never had for me. I hated him. I hated myself. The icing on the cake is he doesn't know about the tape, or that I know what has been going on behind my back. I was going to forgive him how pathetic am I. Out of the blue, he came to my apartment declaring that he needed to brake up with me.

I am devastated at how he ended our relationship. I know I should not be upset about it. I mean, thanks to one of the members on the debate team, I am now the proud owner of a tape featured his trysts with these girls. At least I knew without a doubt where I stood in our relationship this whole time. If I so desired, I could even use this tape to blackmail him. I thought Justin and I were on the fast track to marriage, despite our many problems. I kept telling myself, he wouldn't stick around this long if he didn't care. I should have seen it coming, especially with his little jabs about my love handles and his "back that booty up" comments he made. Granted I did just lose sixty-five pounds and now have a flat tummy. It is still soft. My best features are my striking blue green eyes and my solid double D breasts. This and following paragraph would be a good area to develop the character's emotions, fears, and self-image. You have a great start at acknowledging the need for her to reaffirm her own worth, but just how hard it is. I'm really glad you've included this into your novel, because a lot of people tend to neglect this important aspect.

My hundred and seventy-five-pound body is jam packed into a five six frame. It is no wonder why my self esteem is ten feet under the ground. I have been trying hard lately to reaffirm my self-worth by taking different kinds of dance classes, like pole dancing or belly dancing, but with Justin calling me every name he can think of me as he packs his car, I can feel all my hard work starting to crumble. A gallon of cookie dough ice cream is calling my name, but after stuffing my face with the Chinese food that could feed a family of four, with leftovers for days to spare, I feel sick at the idea that I even want to eat more. Maybe he's right ... Maybe it's me ... I'm not good enough. Do I really blame him for leaving? I try to stop these thoughts from taking control, but not a single positive affirmation is able to compete with the harsh words I've been hearing for weeks. I'm so caught up in these thoughts that I didn't hear my best friend walk up behind me.

"Hallelujah. Lexi, we are going to party tonight," Dakota hollers. Dakota never liked Justin. She was always telling me there was something off with him, but she could never pin point what it was. When I showed the tape to her all she did was stand there in shock with her hand over her mouth. This was not something I could keep from my best friend she would know how to help meemotionally. Everyone needs a tell it like it is friend even when you don't want to hear it. I know this break up is for the best because emotionally he was tearing me apart. I also know if Justin found out about either the tape or that I watched it, there was going to be hell to pay, both emotionally and physically.

"Lexi, didn't I tell you he wasn't good enough for you? This just proves it," Dakota states smugly. "The bastard could have waited until after finals were over before he broke up with you. He is just mad you have been spending so much time getting our new business together and not spending time with him. Girl, we have our whole life ahead of us. Our college lives, including your relationship with him will be over after this next week. He is just messing with you because he wants you to fail."

I know she is right, but I am in survival mode and I don't want to think about it. I have finals and I need to pack for the first event we are doing right after we finish school. I just am at the point where I don't want to think about him ever again. Put it out of my mind and he will just disappear.

"I totally agree with you but, I am really tired of being just one of the guys. Do you know how frustrating it is to watch you go on dates and I only get to "'hang out?'" I want a man to cherish me. He doesn't have to kiss the ground I walk on but at least kiss me and mean it." I sighed towards Dakota. "Also I need to have the guy only be kissing me; I do not want to share a man. Seeing that stupid video with him and those other girls made that painfully clear. I am never going to share a man with anyone else. Period."

"I totally understand and feel the same way. None of the guys from the North West are good enough for us" Dakota beams. "We are about to embark on the greatest journey of our lives. There will be a plentiful amount of sexy men who are going to be single, and ready to mingle."I sigh. I wasn't ready to mingle by any means. I start crying and before I know it, I unleash all the thoughts in my head. "Just always dangled romance and affection in front of my face. It was almost like a game to him. He was all words and no action, promising it would be just the two of us. He'd always say we'd be able to spend time together. You know, simple stuff like cuddling up while watching Netflix" I pause. "He never did spend time with me. Most nights he was too caught up playing video games to even notice I existed. That is unless he wanted to get off, and I had no choice in the situation." Dakota stares at me and she looks as if she is about to say something. It's probably some words of encouragement, but I don't let her talk. I finally tell her what's been weighing down on me the most. "Dakota, do you know how sick it made me to hear him say to those girls on the tape, 'tell me how you like it?'. I was disgusted. That's what he'd say to me when he ... " "Lexi – " I recover with a weak smile. "And don't get me started on his fascination with not wanting to wear protection."

"Lexi, why are we even talking about that looser?" Dakota called out, "just chalk it up to a lesson learned."

Of course, it was a lesson learned. I went to the doctor last week to make sure Justin didn't leave me with a parting gift. Luckily, I dodged a bullet there. Sometimes I wonder if he got anyone pregnant, but that is as far as that little thought ever goes. Not my problem anymore. From now on any man I am with will not only wear a condom during sex, they will respect and love me the way I deserve. And I will never have to hear the words tell me how you like it ever again.

"You're right D, but if a guy like Justin doesn't want to be with me, then who will? I want a family, my own home, and I would like to have a man who loves me for me. I want someone who wants to share his time with me." I breathe. I'm getting carried away again, and I can see Dakota getting ready to lecture me again. Before she gets the chance, I say as upbeat as I can, "I want to forget Justin even exists and get ready for the next chapter of my life. We are going to finish school. We are going to pack up my Range Rover with all our stand and head to our first event planning job in Chicago!" I sigh.

The next week flew by in a blur, Dakota and I finished our finals, packed up our dorm room and we hit the road. We had given ourselves a week to get from Vancouver, Washington to Chicago. We said a prayer, crossed our fingers, and headed east out of Vancouver. We watched in the rearview mirror as we left the city we called home for the last four years. We were on our way to the rest of our lives. Together we could do anything. There was nothing stopping us or anyone holding us down.

After a stop in Spokane to visit our parents we are on our way to Chicago. We are hoping to make it to Billings, Montana before we stop for the night. An hour passes after stopping in Helena Montana for gas and snacks. Once we hop back in and start the truck, we notice something is different. My truck is making a funny noise.

"D, did you hear that?" I question, startled."

"Huh, what did you say?" she asks sheepishly?

"I think my truck just made a funny noise. Did you hear it?"

Before Dakota can say anything, my truck seizes up and I have to coast it to the side of the road. I reach up to the cubby hole where I keep my cell phone. "Please let me have cell service," I mumble, looking up to the sky.

Well here I am in the middle of nowhere and I haven't seen another car on the road since we left Helena. This is a great way to start this journey.

"I can't believe this is happening, I have to update my status," Dakota declares!

Dakota is alwaystweeting about our daily adventures. Her phone is always glued to her hand It's what she's best at, which is why she is president of social media for DaLexa Party Planning. So far we are up to three hundred "likes," and almost as many followers. I think they are just trying to follow us to see how we do with our first party.

"Yes" I do a mental fist pump into the air because I didn't think there would be any sort of cell service. I actually have cell coverage in the middle of nowhere. At least we won't have to wait out here like sitting ducks hoping for a stranger to stop and help us, or worse, walk to the nearest town.

After hanging up with the tow truck company Dakota and I wait for the tow truck to arrive. Time crawled by. "Hey D, do you have any chocolate left? My stomach is about to start growling. I knew I should have grabbed some the last time we stopped" I asked?

"I just put the last piece I had in my mouth, sorry."I must be hallucinating, it looked like a red Porsche just sped by. That is weird, Justin has the same car. Too bad it went by so fast I know it's pathetic, but I actually remember is plate number. Time to focus, I tell myself. First I need to get this truck to the shop and figure out the damage so we can get back on the road. I should also figure out how a brand-new car straight from the factory can break down a week after it was given to me.

My vehicle is my dream truck. It was my college graduation present from my parents. It is a 2014 Land Range Rover Sport edition. Silver with black interior leather so soft it feels like a newborns bottom wrapped in silk. This car is loaded with every gadget known to man. It sits on 20" chromed wheels. It was everything I needed, and the greatest gift ever. Did I mention how much I love this car? ... And now it's broken down on the side of the road making a funny noise. Hopefully it won't take too long to get it fixed. I am hoping it is just a loose screw or a wire. We cannot screw this party up in Chicago or DaLexa Party Planning will be out of business before it even gets off the ground. Assuming my bad luck doesn't follow me from college, it may just be a loose wire or a quick replacement.

After what seems like an eternity the tow truck shows up, and to my surprise another vehicle pulls in right behind the tow truck. I am so happy the dispatcher told them there are two of us and had them send another vehicle, because sometimes when you tell them there are two people they think it is okay to scrunch all three of you in the cab of the tow truck. Thankfully, all three of us wont have to sit across the tow truck bench seat for however long it takes us to get to the nearest town. I am grateful I don't have to sit next to the stinky tow truck driver.

Dakota and I were standing away from the two vehicles a couple feet down the highway trying to stay out of the way while my truck is getting loaded onto the back of the tow truck. I'm observing the process when the hair on the back of my neck stands up. I have this feeling someone is watching me, but whenever I look around there is never anyone besides the four of us around.

Finally I ask, "Dakota, do you see anyone around here besides the tow truck guys?"

"No, Lexi I don't. Why do you ask?"

"I feel like we are being watched, and the hair on the back of my neck is standing up, I guess I am going crazy."I feel really dumb asking Dakota if she sees anyone when we're clearly alone. I'm probably just stressed about my car and letting my worries get the best of me.

All of a sudden Dakota grabs my arm and my attention is being torn from my sense of uneasiness to reality. As I look at Dakota, she is staring at the guy who is driving the second vehicle. It's the one we are supposed to be riding in. I mean, she's not just staring. She is standing there with her mouth wide open, drool dripping on her chin, and her eyes are bugging out so far her Maui Jim sunglasses can not even hide them. To make matters worse after traveling all day, both of us have our hair thrown up in a messy bun on top of our heads. I guess that goes to show us to always make sure we look presentable – even if you're traveling in the middle of nowhere. Just like my mamma always said, 'Make sure you always wear a clean pair of underwear. You know, in case of an emergency.'

Both guys make their way over to us after my truck is loaded onto the flat bed. The tow truck driver reaches out to shake our hands.

"Hi, I am Dennis, I will oversee getting your truck back to the shop in one piece," He says with a slick side grin.

The second guy reaches his hand out, "And I am Jaxson James, you will be trusting your lives in my hands until we reach the garage in Shelby." Again with a slick side grin, What is with these guys? What is with those smiles? While looking at Dakota I see he has stars twinkling in his deep gray eyes.

"If you guys think you're funny then I suggest you don't quit your day jobs," I state sarcastically as I reach out to shake their hands.

"Oh, by the way, I am Alexus but my friends call me Lexi. And this lady to my left is Dakota, but we all call her D."

"Hello." Dakota says so quietly that I can barely hear her. I want to tell D to roll her tongue up, but that would probably embarrass her.

CHAPTER THREE

ROYCE

"H ello, Double J Ranch. Can I help you?"

"Yes, I am looking for Royce."

"I am sorry. He is in a meeting. Can I take a message?"

"Tell him Justin Kramer called, and we have an old business deal to hash out.""Yes, sir. I will let Royce know you called. Have I nice day," Grace, my receptionist replies, as she hangs up the receiver.

I am having a great day, that is until I walk in to the office where my assistant is finishing up a phone message when I walk in the office. The next thing I know all hell is breaking loose. "If I heard right, my assistant just took a message from Justin Kramer"Man, I haven't heard that name in five years. Five peaceful, drama-free years. I wonder what he wants now. I thought we were done with that guy and his crazy family. I suppose the only way to find out is to call him back. Granted, a conversation with Justin isn't something any sane person would look forward to. After everything happened with the lawsuit between the ranch and his family, I made sure to put in additional security measures. When I dial his number, I make sure that our call is being recording. You can never be too cautious with the Kramer family.

"Royce, it is so good to hear from you," Justin laughs.

"Cut the crap Justin. What do you want? We haven't heard from you or your family in years and now you are wanting to chit chat? I don't buy it."

"Well since we are cutting the bull and heading straight to the chase, I have a business proposition for you."

"Not interested. You're wasting my time and your breath," I yell.

"Are you still mad about the dog breeding incident?"

"Nope. We, as in the ranch, have moved on and I suggest you do the same."

"Are you not the least bit curious about what my proposition is going to be?" Justin questions?

"No. Now this conversation is over. Goodbye!"

I slam the phone down a little harder than I planned.

Well, hopefully that will be the last time anyone in this family will see or hear of Justine Kramer again.

I called my brother as soon as I can. He had sent me a text and he even tried to call me while I was on the phone with Justin. I read the text saying he was going with the tow truck to pick up a brand-new Range Rover that had broke down on the side of the road. I can't believe a brand-new car would break down, but I guess it could be a defect with a part from the manufacturer.

Mine is brand new as well and it is in pristine condition.

CHAPTER FOUR

LEXI

When we reach the garage, I ask, "How long is my truck going to be out of commission?"

"Well pretty lady it will probably be a few weeks, and that is only because we don't carry the parts required to fix it." Jaxson explains. "If you drove a Ford or a Chevy we could have you on your way in no time, but these Range Rovers tend to require more time."

"Do you happen to know what is wrong with it? Because seriously this car is brand new. I have only had it a week."Well," Jaxson begins hesitantly, "before Dennis and I loaded it onto the flatbed, we checked all your fluids and it seems you have no transmission fluid." Jaxson pauses, likely noticing that my eyes are wide and my mouth dropping. He continues, "It seems your hoses have been tampered with."

My mind is reeling. How could this have happened. I have had cars before, and I know there is no way for things like this to happen on their own. He's right, my vehicle must have been tampered with. But who would sabotage my car? I can't think of anyone who would dislike me that much. I mean, I can't even think of anyone who had any sort of ill will towards me. Have you ever seen this on any other vehicles? I mean, I really don't want to think that anyone's been messing with my car, but... from what you're telling me, I'm guessing this probably wasn't an accidental break down."

"No I have never seen this before, and I believe your brand-new car has been tampered with. Someone apparently wanted you to suffer major car problems. I am going to have to go through this with a fine-tooth comb and make sure I don't miss anything."

"Thanks Jaxson." This doesn't put my mind at ease, in fact that it makes me think that maybe Justin did tamper with my car, I mean I thought I saw his car pass by us at a high rate of speed. No, Justin couldn't have done it. He was no where near my car, I had only gotten it for graduating and by then he had already broken up with me. There is no way that he knew what I drive. I am just overthinking it. It has to be that I got a lemon and its a manufacturing defect. It has to be.

"Is there any place around here for us to eat?" Dakota asks. "We haven't eaten anything decent since early this morning and we were about to find a place to stop and eat before the car made its way to the side of the road."

Hallelujah! She finally speaks. I mean at first glance I didn't think Jaxson was that great looking. Now, I have more time to look at him up close he is more handsome than I thought. Go get him Dakota I am silently rooting on my best friend.

Jaxson stands 6'3" and has a broad chest with an eight pack of abs that form a little nice tight V shape that runs an arrow pointing down towards his manhood. That is behind the loose-fitting jeans hanging dangerously low on his hips and tight butt.

Jaxson starts to tell us about a diner in the heart of town. I am not paying attention to anything that is coming out of Jaxson's mouth, because with all this new overwhelming information my mind has stopped. What do I do, I can't ignore it, but I don't want to tell my parents either. It is not like they would come to my rescue anyway. I am supposed to be an adult now. Not a burden.

The next thing that I hear is D blurting out, "Wanna join us? We can get to know each other better. Maybe we can even become friends? You know since we are kind of stuck here for weeks. We might as well know at least one person in this town."She cocks her head and blinks, an innocent, flirtatious smile spreading. My friend always has to be the life of the party. Dakota can make friends anywhere so why am I not surprised by her flirting with Jaxson.

What is she talking about joining us? What have I missed? I am miles away in my own world. Do I ask what is going on? As I continue to listen to their conversation I figure out what is going on. She is hungry, and since she likes Jaxson then why not invite him. I mean he did miss lunch helping us out. Much to my surprise, I hear Jaxson say, "Yeah, sure. Not a problem! Let me call my brother at the ranch. Maybe he could join us."

My eyes are now popping out of my head. Did he just say brother? Oh, please Heavenly Father let him be hot!Dakota can't be the only one getting luck on this little adventure of ours, I think while suppressing a giggle

When Jaxson walks out of his office he has a weird look on his face. Me being me I ask him "What's up? What's wrong?"Jaxson must have decided we weren't too bad, because he let us know he was feeling a little concerned that his brother didn't answer. "It's strange. He always answers his cell."

Again, me being me, my heart sinks because I want to meet the brother. I was silently praying that he would be hot like his brother Jaxson.

CHAPTER FIVE

ROYCE

I take my cell phone out of my pocket and look at it. I missed another call from Jaxson. Waiting for the call to go through to my brother, I miss the open greeting of hello on his end. "Jaxson, I just got off the phone. I had a really weird call from Justin Kramer."

"No way! What is that scum bag up to these days?"

"I have no clue, but he said he had a business proposition for us. I pretty much hung up on him. I wasn't in the mood to listen to him."

"Good I never really liked that guy or his parents. No matter how much money they have, they will never have the class like mom and dad did. Thankfully. they taught us to have that same class and respect for others, especially in our business deals."

"Well forget about it. I just towed in that brand new Range Rover into the shop, and the two ladies and I are heading over to the diner for lunch."

"Why would a brand new Range Rover need a tow,

anyway? I was reading your texts. I was wondering what happened."

"From the quick glance I took before getting it all towed back to town, it looks like the transmission hose was sabotaged. There was no transmission fluid in the truck," Jaxson says flatly.

"Seriously?" I exhale. "Well, I'll head over to the diner and meet up with you guys. Remember the rules, Jaxson. Don't let onto these girls about our money until I can run a background check on them.""I know bro, but I am telling you these girls are legit. They just graduated from college and this car of hers is brand new. It shouldn't have broken down. I'll text you all of their info later. We'll get to the bottom of this. I'm sure it's nothing." Since I have nothing really pressing that needs to be done I decide to go over to the diner and see for myself what Jaxson is talking about.

CHAPTER SIX

LEXI

Jaxson's cell phone starts buzzing so he stepps away from Dakota and me to answer it. I must look on the bright side of things, I tell myself. I still might get to meet Jaxson's brother, which is important, especially since I don't think Dakota is going to be leaving Jaxson's side anytime soon. Hopefully she will spend some time with me too. so we can brainstorm ideas for the event we are hired to do.

I know there's more important things to brainstorm over – like who would tamper with my car? And why? I refuse to let myself think too much about that, though. It sends my blood pumping and makes my hands shake. Maybe it's nothing. In an effort to not dwell on the frightening events in my life, I decide to think of the cute tow truck guy and his brother.

"Well, ladies let's go and get some food. We have all had a long afternoon."

"Alright, let's go. I guess you're driving since my car is

out of commission," I playfully joke.

"I can do that," Jaxson replies. "Dakota why don't you have a car with you guys?"I gasp as quietly as I can, but I can't stop myself from thinking – is the real reason she doesn't like to drive going to come out? A few minutes of awkward silence pass, and I'm just about ready to interrupt with a change of subject, but then I hear her say, "Um, I really don't like to drive." She says it with a slight smile that doesn't touch her eyes.

"Oh, okay. Well let's climb into the truck and we can head to get some of the best grub in town." Jaxson says as we climb into this huge monster Dodge Ram 2500 king cab truck with chrome wheels. It too was fully loaded with all the extras, I let Dakota sit up front with Jaxson while I tried to collect my thoughts about my life, my car and why it was sabotaged, and this feeling I couldn't shake. Nothing is making sense in my world. Just two weeks ago, I was stressing about getting a good grade on my exam. Now, here I am – a girl who's ex-boyfriend who was recorded cheating on her, about to let go of that terrible past and embark on the rest of my life. I can't even get away from any of this, because I'm stuck in some town because someone messed with my Range Rover. How is this even possible? I didn't think anyone would want to do this to me, but apparently, I am wrong.

As Jaxson drives towards the diner, he seems to relax. He flashes his killer smile, you know the one girls get all mushy over, and Dakota giggles. I was watching them when they did the initial hand shake and both jumped back from the shock that coursed through both of their bodies. Not everyone gets that spark. It's one of those things that is so rare, it's as if it's a once in a lifetime moment. It's entertaining to watch how careful the two are around each other now, avoiding an accidental brush of the fingers or bumping into each other.

CHAPTER SEVEN

LEXI

While walking into the diner, all the air comes rushing out of my body. The hair on the back of my neck is now sticking up and not in the good way.

I am thinking to myself that this can't be good. I'm glancing around the diner when suddenly my chest feels as if it's being crushed by a ton of bricks. There in the corner red vinyl booth sits Justin.

I can't move. All I can do is put my arms around myself and collapse to the ground. My mind is racing with all the possibilities of why he is here and if it was his car I saw on the highway.

Dakota rushes over to me asking me frantically. "Lexi what is wrong? What is going on?"

After she asks all those questions I don't even have time to answer her before she hears his laugh. Next thing I hear is Justin's voice as he is walking towards me. "Lexi, baby," he says. "it is so wonderful to see you! Have you put on a few pounds since I left you?" Justin kneels and whispers in my ear, "Tell me how you like it, baby." My skin crawls as his breath hits my ear and those awful words enter my mind. It's like it's only the two of us now, but not in a romantic way. In my mind, I am alone with the man who destroyed me. My hands are trembling. I shove them in my pocket. That simple sentence brings back a countless memories filled with pain – nights where despite degrading my body and telling me how fat I am, he would use me like a doll. I know I'm not exactly sexy, but I'm not huge. America has the wrong thinking. I am a healthy 5'6" woman with curves in all the right places. So, what? I will never be a size two, and I am fine with that. I did lose over sixty pounds and I finally like the way I look. And then Justin came along and ruined everything, just like he always does. I physically can't move from the ground as Justin leaves the diner. Now I am embarrassed I'm still rooted to my spot on the floor of the diner. Granted I'm not physically hurt, but my mental and emotional state has been shot to hell. There is another commotion and before I knew what is happening, a tall, dark, and incredibly sexy stranger is crouching down before me and helping me to my feet, like I weigh nothing at all. I mumble a quick "thank you" and run to the nearest booth hoping no one will bother me with a million questions about the guy who made me fall and become immobile.

My solitude is short lived when Jaxson, Dakota, and the mystery man all come to the booth where I am trying to hide. They all sit down.

"Apparently, I am not the only person who is having a bad day," the mystery man says.

As I look up to the sexy voice, I get a good look at him. He has dark hair, with waves, and great big hazel eyes. From what I can tell, he is built well. He has broad shoulders that taper off down towards his waist. I am guessing he has to be at least six foot three inches, since he towers over my body and picked me up like I weighed nothing at all. Finally, after gawking at him, I begin to questioned the mystery man. "I don't mean to be rude but who are you?" I am starting not to care who he is since he is such a hottie but I still need to ask. I just got out of a relationship that turned bad. I mean come on, this man isn't even in my league. Asking was the only way to get information. I am starting to realize I should have been asking questions a long time ago, and maybe I would not be in the mess my life is turning out to be.

He gives me the same semi-sly smile that Jaxson gave us when we first met him. All I wanted to do was put my lips on his because they looked so soft, but I doubted he want to be with me, I had just made a fool of myself. I had just made a total fool of myself back there. Why would he even begin to be interested in me? I think I need to learn when not to doubt myself. I feel as if my life would be very different if I could start trusting in my abilities.

"Oh, I am sorry. Where are my manners? I am Royce James, brother to Jaxson here." Royce smiles and then asks,"Jaxson, who are these two lovely ladies' you are sitting with,"

"Oh, my bad bro. These two ladies are Alexus and Dakota." Jaxson says to his brother as he points each of us out.

"Oh crap." Now my face is exceptionallyred. "Sorry I didn't mean to come on strong. I was just wondering and normally when I get nervous I turn into a total smart ass. Now can I go hide in my shell, or maybe a hotel room?" I just want to get away from everyone. Too much stuff has gone down in the last few weeks especially within the last twenty-four hours. I thought I couldn't get any more embarrassed when I glance over at Jaxson and D. Both of them are laughing so hard, they are almost falling of the booth.

"By any chance, can we get the spot-light off me and just have lunch? I am starving," I question.

"I am sorry, Lexi. Yes, we will order and just get to know each other more. Dakota, to answer your question before about a place to stay in the town, there is an inn. It's just up the road. I thought I couldn't get any more embarrassed when I glance over at Jaxson and D. Both of them are laughing so hard, they are almost falling of the booth.

"Wait, how did you know his name?" I ask Jaxson

"Oh um, Dakota explained to me what was going on you when he came up to and you ... " he trails off and gives me a sad look. We both know what happened next. "Okay, then. Thank you, Dakota, for letting a complete stranger know my life story. At least I don't have to answer a thousand questions, I guess."

I am just happy Royce doesn't know anything about this.

"Lexi, please don't be mad at me. I just knew you wouldn't want to talk about it. Just like you kept quiet when I was asked about driving." Dakota whispers to me.

"Anyway, Jaxs what are the chances he is still in town?" I ask.

"Jaxs?" Royce raises his eyebrows.

Jaxson just shakes his head in a don't-ask fashion.

Royce and Jaxson go up and pay the bill for lunch. We are now on our way to the inn up the street. Hopefully, I will not run into Justin during the rest of my stay here. Yeah, like that is going to happen. I specifically have this feeling he is going to be staying around town. Why can't men leave me alone? First they only want to be my friend and treat me like one of the guys. If they want to be with me, then when they leave me they never actually leave. I feel like shouting, but I don't want to scare anyone. This is starting to get old real fast.

CHAPTER EIGHT

ROYCE

When I pull up into the diner parking lot, I can tell there is a commotion going on in the entry way. I start to wonder what the heck is going on. As I approach the scene, I notice what appears to be a female sitting on the floor of the diner. Why would she be sitting on the floor? I wait and see what is about to play out. I can a patient man on occasion, and in this case, it may pan out well for me.

As soon as I see Justin walk over to the female on the floor, he brushes his finger to move her hair out of her face and then whispers something in her ear. That is when she goes ridged. Well, now I know this is crazy, but every cell in my body is telling me I need to protect her. I know just how dangerous Justin can be, and it's clear he has a traumatizing effect on this girl.

Justin walks out of the diner and smiling at me as he walks by. Oh, what an ass! Now that I know he is in town, my feelings of unease are much greater. I am almost certain that he is behind that car breaking down on the side of the road. Maybe I am being paranoid, but I know what he is capable of.

I walk right by my brother but we catch each other's eyes saying that we are thinking the same thing. I scoop up the lady off the floor and whisper. "Apparently I am not the only person who is having a bad day."

I notice the goose bumps on her arms. It's not cold in here. As soon as I sit her down, she runs to a booth in the back of the diner. I watch her knowing she felt too good in my arms to let her get away that easy. I quickly realize these are the girls that my brother picked up – because their vehicle had been tampered with. I'm even more convinced Justin and their car problems are not a coincidence.

After lunch, Jaxson drives Lexi and Dakota to the inn. I decided to ride along. I can't get this woman out of my head, and I have only just found out her name is Alexus, but she prefers Lexi and her friend, Dakota, but she also goes by a nickname. It's not that long before they've assigned a nickname to my brother as well.

We go the short distance to the inn, and no one says a word during the drive. Jaxson and I don't want to give away the fact that we know Justin. Dakota and Lexi clearly don't want to admit that this guy might still be in town. Especially, Lexi. She can barely utter his name.

Pulling into the Inn owned by Iris, a nice old lady who happens to be the town gossip. I notice that it seems as if the air in the cab of the truck vanishes, and Lexi goes still. Apparently, she spots the same car I see. We both know who the owner of it is.

CHAPTER NINE

LEXI

I can't go in there. I can't ask for a room because his car is parked almost directly in front of the doors just off to the right, but I must go because I don't have anywhere else to sleep. I am cursing this small town right now, and it's not even their fault I have an ex boyfriend who seems to keep wanting to make my life less than pleasant. Well I guess it is time to put the "big girl panties" on and face the music.

Royce, Jaxson, Dakota and I all walk into the inn. I stand in between Royce and Jaxson, and Dakota is on the other side of Jaxson. It is my own little protection shield. We are greeted by a lovely older lady with permed hair, soft eyes, and a professional smile.

"Hello, welcome to my lovely inn, I am Iris, how may I help you girls today?"

"Um yes, my friend and I need a room," Dakota tells Iris. "Also, we need to be as far away as possible from your guest named Justin Kramer please. That would really be appreciated."

"Oh I see, um let me see what we have available. It looks like we do have a room. How long are you two lovely ladies planning on staying in town?"

Dakota looks at me and I look at Jaxson, who finally says, "About a week or two."

"Very well" Iris says. "You two will be in room one, which is located just down the hall and to your left." Jaxson and Dakota step aside as I fill out paperwork and pay for the room. Royce remains by my side, his posture tense, and I can't help but wonder if it's because of me. Did I say something wrong?"Jaxson," I hear Dakota say, "would you like to go to dinner with me tonight? I think Alexus just wants to hang out in the room and veg out."I look over at them, curious as to how Jaxson will respond.

"Sure, that sounds great. I need to take care of some business at the shop and then talk to my brother about some things that are going on down at the ranch.

I will pick you up here at six thirty tonight."

"That sounds great." Dakota smiles.

CHAPTER TEN

ROYCE

Iris is a smart lady and she is starting to put two and two together. I just hope she doesn't spread any gossip about Lexi and Dakota around town. After making sure the girls made it to their room without incident, Jaxson and I leave for the rest of the day. It is odd, but I just have this feeling I need to stay close and keep an eye on Lexi.

"What is going on here, Jaxson? Do you like Dakota? I thought you just met her this morning."

"Yeah, I did, but there is something about her, bro. I cannot put my finger on it, but something is happening. I wasn't even supposed to be in the shop when the call came through, but, it just so happened that when dispatch said there were two girls involved, I decided to go along. I didn't want them to have to squeeze in the cab of the tow truck. Now I am happy with my choice."

"Yeah, I get that. It's kind of weird, huh? I mean, you're clearly into Dakota and here I am with the strangest sense that I need to protect Lexi, especially now that we know she's associated with Justin."

"Dude, did you not just witness the same lady on the ground paralyzed with fear because of his touch and whatever the hell he whispered to her?" Royce scolds.

"Okay, I get where you are coming from. Let's go and do some investigating into this. But for now, we keep quiet about knowing Justin. We willjust play along and, fill them in when needed. Sadly, I don't think Justin Kramer is going to be leaving us anytime soon. Especially since we don't know if this has anything to do with not listening to his business proposition, or it could have something to do with Lexi."

"I have to agree with you bro."

Jaxson drops me off at the diner so I can pick up my truck. After starting up the engine, I follow him back to the ranch to see if anything has come back for the background check.

Thanks to our connections to law enforcement, we start to dig and first we find Dakota.

Name: Dakota Smith, Age: 21

Hometown: Spokane, WA,

Relationship status: Single GPA: 3.9.

"Dang, Royce, Dakota is very smart. I wonder why she doesn't have much of a background though. I have no idea who her parents are."

After a few more minutes, Lexi's information pops up.

Name Alexus Green, Age: 22,

Hometown: Spokane, WA,Relationship Status: Single GPA: 3.95, Parents: Josh and Carol Green.

"So is Lexi, apparently. She wanted to work while in school so she wouldn't have the student loans, but her parents only wanted her to concentrate on her education."

"Royce none of this is getting us anywhere, we don't know why Lexi was or is with Justin, and this doesn't explain why a brand-new car would have a slice through a hose and no transmission fluid in it.""Do you think there's any way he's connected to that?" I ask hesitantly. "You never know with the Kramer family. For now, let's not jump to any conclusions. This could all just be one huge coincidence."

Lost in thought I am trying to put this puzzle together but nothing is making sense. There must be a reason for all of this, and I am going to figure this all out.

"Dude are you listening to me?" Jaxson roars.

"No, not really. Isn't that your phone ringing?"

Jaxson answers, putting it on speaker phone. "Hello?"

"Hey Jaxson. This is Dakota, from earlier."

"Oh hey, what's up I wasn't expecting to hear from you so soon. Is there something wrong?"

"No, nothing is wrong I am just worried about Lexi, I don't think she should be left here alone. Do you think your brother could hang out with her while we are out on our date?" She sounds so hesitant to ask. It's cute.

"Dakota, Royce is listening, I have you on speaker phone so you basically just asked him yourself," Jaxson replies chuckling.

"Hey Dakota. Sure, I can keep Lexi company tonight. I didn't have anything else planned. What time were you going to be leaving with Jaxson?"

"Six thirty."

"I will head over there a little after that to see if she would like to join me for dinner. I agree with you that she shouldn't be left alone. We all saw how she reacted when that guy came up to her in the diner."

"Yeah, I don't know what that was all about, but it can't be safe for her. Thanks, Royce, you are the best. You too Jaxson. See you tonight," Dakota says.

After Jaxson hangs up the phone I ask him, "So do you know what you two are doing yet?"

"Yeah, I was just going to bring her back to my place on the ranch, and have dinner and get to know each other. I am not planning taking her back to the Inn, so either you have to stay at the inn with Lexi or bring her to your house. She could sleep in a guest room or you may get lucky as well."

"I doubt she will want to sleep with me, but yeah, I can have dinner prep done. So, no matter what time we come back to the house, it won't take that long to cook. Oh, and maybe under the circumstances, you should text Dakota to grab her bathroom bag or whatever else Lexi might need. She is going to be safer here than with that flimsy lock on her door at the inn. Even though I doubt she will be happy about it. She's probably going to think we're trying to force her into something."

"Okay I will get you that bag before you head back to the Inn to get Lexi," Jaxson states.

Are we doing the right thing? I don't want Lexi to take any of this the wrong way, but I need to keep her safe. In less than 20 minutes she has gotten under my skin. I have this strange feeling that Lexi is the woman I am supposed to be with. She reminds me of Mom. I know it may have seemed like Lexi was overreacting when she collapsed on the floor, but I saw the intense pain in her eyes. I also saw her stand up tall and pull herself together in mere minutes. She is a strong woman. She is such a spitfire and doesn't seem to back down from a fight, no matter how she is feeling. I have a feeling that she won't take crap from anyone, including me.

CHAPTER ELEVEN

LEXI

What a crappy day! I just want to take a walk, clear my head and call my family like we had agreed upon. What are the odds that I would run into Justin here of all places? I might be able to understand Chicago. He could have gotten a job there, but here in the middle of nowhere? That can't be a fluke.

I don't think that it's possible unless he was following me. I thought I saw his flashy car speeding by us on the highway, but I kept telling myself that Justin isn't the only person with a flashy car. I mean, maybe it wasn't him. Maybe it was someone else. It is the highway after all, right? I'm lost in thought when my cellphone rings.

"Hello Momma. Well, no we are not in Billings Montana, we had a little bit of car trouble and we are in Shelby, Montana. I don't know what happened to the car it started making noises and so we pulled off to the side of the road, luckily we had cell service and were able to call for a tow."Concerned, my mother asks if I have had lunch yet and a safe place to stay while my car is repaired.

"Yes, momma we ate, I found some place to stay, and I have capable people working on it. It might take a while since we are in such a small town and not a lot of people drive fancy cars like the one you and daddy bought me. I will talk to you guys later and keep you updated, since I know you will worry. I love you Mom, goodbye."

With my mind running all the scenarios, I decided it was a good idea to take a walk. I wasn't paying attention to what I was doing. I nearly jump when I hear a voice say, "Hey, fatso. Watch where you're going, stupid bitch." I spin around and sure enough I see Justin. For a second, I start to feel myself freeze, and I am afraid I will collapse just like I did at the diner. Before my legs start to buckle, I am overcome with a surge or anger. How dare he? Who even does this? Before I know what I'm doing, I hear my voice start yelling all the thoughts I've kept inside. "What is wrong with you? I am not fat! You are an idiot! I can't believe we dated for four years!" I yell back at him.

"Well, it wasn't because you were good in bed. That is for sure, since you just laid there, and your pussy tasted like dog shit." Justin is now screaming this at me while we are still in the middle of the road.

"The only reason I just laid there was because I never wanted you to touch me I was only trying to get through the motions while you used me to get off! Just like when you would go to your little debate competitions." I scream.

His face falls and he turns ghost white. "What are you talking about?"

"Funny you should ask, but one of the females that you used to sleep with while dating me decided to tape you and then showed it to me. It just happened to be the night you did the whole team."

"Well, I had to do something since you were so fat and couldn't do anything but lie in bed while I did all the work."

"I will never be that stupid to let another man use me again. I am glad we are not together anymore, even if I never have another relationship." I tell Justin.

By this time, I am shouting across the road in front of the inn, because I keep trying to get away from him. He just keeps up the shouting match. Man, what people must think of us. Lost in my self-deprecating thoughts, I almost don't hear him screaming anymore, until he says, "No man will ever sleep with you again. No one is going to ever want you. I ruined you, and you will come crawling back to me begging for forgiveness."

"Well thank you for telling me that. Now I will just die alone and you can go sleep with the next thing with legs and fake tits." I turn to head back to my room, losing all my appetite, I'm trying to get to where he can't follow me. Don't cry, don't cry, don't cry. I repeat this mantra so loudly that it's as if my mind is yelling at me.

CHAPTER TWELVE

ROYCE

As I am walking to go see Lexi, I hear yelling coming from the middle of the road before I see her. I don't have to wait long before I can tell who is involved because I can make out the voices perfectly. Lexi is shouting in the middle of the road with Justin. As I get closer, the shouting becomes louder and I can start making out words. I hear Lexi yell, "What is wrong with you! I am not fat! You are an idiot! I can't believe we dated for four years!" Damn I was right it was Lexi who was with that douche bag. Justin isn't as loud and so I can't make out what he is saying back but I could give a guess. Lexi continues "The only reason I just laid there was because I never wanted you to touch me. I was only trying to get through the motions while you used me to get off. Just like when you would go to your little debate competitions." Lexi screaming again. That must have hit a nerve, because Justin didn't look too good after that one. I fight the urge to run over and beat the crap out of Justin. I'm close enough to make sure he doesn't cause any physical harm to Lexi and step in if needed. She's not crumbling this time, though. She is fighting back, and I know how important it is to fight back, so I let her.

The yelling didn't stop there. The last things I hear is "Funny you should ask, but one of the females you used to sleep with while dating me decided to tape you, and then showed it to me. It just happened to be the night you did the whole team. sadly, I would have looked the other way, but I will never be that stupid again. I will never be that stupid to let another man use me again. Well thank you for telling me that. Now I will just die alone and you can go sleep with the next thing with legs and fake tits."Wow. All I can say is, wow! She knows how to hit where it counts, but I know she must be embarrassed. Also, I'm pretty sure she needs someone at this point, but Dakota is already gone. I guess I can step in and see what I can do.

Well, that answers one question I was trying to figure out. She was with Justin but now she is not. That is a great start I think. Baby steps, Royce. Everything will work out if I keep listening and watching what happens while Justin is in town.

CHAPTER THIRTEEN

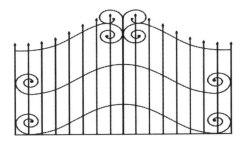

LEXI

exi! Lexi, wait up!" I hear someone in the distance yell, but I don't even turn my head. I don't care. I have to get away. When a very masculine scent washes over me and two very strong arms grabs around my mid-section, I am still fighting and trying to get away. I am almost positive its Justin wanting to keep me around to listen to more sexual insults and fat comments.

"Alexus stop fighting me," Royce whispers in my ear.

Huh?Why is Royce coming to my rescue? Why?I am so confused, but no one hit me over the head. I just want to get away from my personal hell. Sometimes, I feel like I am seeking attention. My parents were never around and I couldn't go to them for help. I think I am just surprised someone came to see if I needed help.

"Lexi it's me Royce. Calm down. He left, so he can't and won't hurt you anymore I promise. Not on my watch."

"Royce, why are you here? Why do you care so much? You don't even know me. For all you know, I might be a psychotic witch and I deserve all the crap he is throwing at me. Anyway, I thought you were back at your ranch working." I question, tears streaming down my cheeks.

My mind keeps reeling and I just can't take it anymore so I slump to the ground. I do not care that I am in the in the road heading back to the inn. It's almost seven o'clock in the evening. I don't think there will be people running to the store, besides I don't even know if the store is open.

Royce squats down so he is eye level with me and says, "No baby girl, I was at my ranch, but after you having that run in with that man at the diner, I decided I was going to come and invite you to dinner. I didn't want you to be alone. Then I saw and heard the way he was talking to you, and well, I couldn't let you run away. Plus, I wanted to get to know you better and to tell you not to listen to a word he is saying."

"Baby girl? Last I checked I was not yours. We hardly know each other. The only pet name you can call me is Lexi." I snap back. I find myself getting angry at this hunk of a man, and it's not even his fault, but I am getting tired of all this drama in my life. I don't have any room in my life or mind for Royce. "Plus, you keep seeing me at my worst, and that cannot be sexy. Just let me go and be alone." I sigh.

"Not going to happen Lexi." Royce says with a wink. "I cannot in good conscience let you go back to your room alone and upset. You need to eat and this is not a request. I don't want you to wake up and be so hungry that you are in pain."

Did I hit my head and not realize it? This isn't happening to me. This must be a dream. Yeah, a dream. I am going to wake up and be back home. I'm sure I haven't even left yet, because that's just my luck.

CHAPTER FOURTEEN

ROYCE

What are you doing here, Royce?" She asks again.
"I was hungry, and I thought you might want to get a bite to eat and have some company."

"No, not really. I just want to go back to the inn and go to sleep."

"Baby girl, you cannot go to bed on an empty stomach."

"For the last time, I am not your baby girl. Besides, I could stand to skip a few meals."

"Sorry, but it is very easy for me to call you baby girl, and If I ever hear you degrade yourself like that again, I will take you over my knee and spank you. Now, are you hungry or no?."

She has a look of fear in her eyes. I think I may have overstepped my hand.

"No really I am not hungry. I just want to go back and get over this bad day."

"I am not letting you go back alone with that guy lurking about."After much convincing, Lexi agrees to let me follow her back to her room at the inn. She is trying everything to make me leave her there alone, but I can be as patient I am stubborn.

When we're in Lexi's room, she sits on one of the beds and I sit on the other. It's quiet for a long time. I think she is eyeing me to make sure I am being honorable with my intentions. Apparently, I have to earn her trust. I decide I'm going to start with asking her questions and finding out who Alexus really is. Once I get her to open-up about herself a little, she seems to relax more. She loves her family, I also find out that she has a sister named McKenna who is about fifteen years older than she is. Her parents were young when they had her, and then decided that they wanted another baby. "So, if I may ask, why aren't you close to your sister?"She pauses for a few minutes before replying, "I don't know. We never liked the same things, and she always seemed caught up in her own life. There was never a place for me in it."I couldn't imagine not being close my brother. Jaxson and I, are only eleven months apart. We can look and sometimes act like twins. My mom was crazy in love with my dad, and they couldn't keep their hands off each other even after having us kids. Until the day they died, they had weekly "dates." More often than not it ended up being multiple times a week. That is the kind of relationship I am wanting. I know we live in a hook up culture, but I've always craved something a bit more real. Losing my parents taught me that life is short, and I don't want to spend my life chasing after a temporary happiness. I want something that lasts, perhaps even beyond the grave.

I am way past hungry, so I finally say, "Are you ready for dinner? It's after ten o'clock."

"I really don't think anything will be open."

"Um, well I know one place that is open. They only cater to certain clientele."

"Like what clientele are we talking about? How am I supposed to dress?""Oh, you look just fine," I say with a wink. Her eyes get big, and I know she's about to lecture me or make some demeaning comment about herself. Before she gets the chance to say anything, I smile and say, "Let's go. It's about a twenty-minute drive from here."

CHAPTER FIFTEEN

LEXI

I learn a lot about Royce while we sit and talk in my room at the inn. He is the protector of his family and his close friends. So why is he protecting a virtual stranger? If he keeps this up he is going to irritate me in a way no man ever has – by caring enough about me to make sure I'm safe.

Of course, Royce was not having any of my stubborn attitude, it would have been way too easy. Ever since Royce found me in the diner, he seems to have the same distaste for Justin, like I do.

Yes, I had just lost a good amount of weight, but I didn't do it because Justin was making fun of me. I was doing it because I was tired of being and feeling the way I was. I am going to make changes for the better, and make myself happy, and to me that is all that matters. At this point in my life, I'm not sure what happiness is or who I am anymore. I feel as if I changed to fit into what Justin wanted me to be, and it still wasn't good enough for him. I know that's why he went to the debate team to fill a void. Well since he is the one who dumped me why won't he leave me alone? These thoughts keep going over and over in my head.

Time to make the best of this situation. This is going to have to be my motto now that I can't and do not want to get rid of Royce. It might be good to have him around. I just need to see where this is going to take me. Moreover, I need to remember I still have a job to do, because now I refuse to fail. I have people counting on me, and this is going to jump start mine and Dakota's careers.

CHAPTER SIXTEEN

ROYCE

Man you ask a lot of questions, you know that? No, you do not need to change, and we are going to a place that has an all-night kitchen to certain people." I say with a wink.

"To certain people? What is this? Is this a club of some sort? I don't want to get anyone kicked out because I look like a slob. And if I must go, I will have some fruit or maybe even a carrot stick," Lexi was her arms in the air.

"A carrot stick? That is all you want a carrot stick?" I remark.

"Well no, that is not what I necessarily want, but it is all I really need. I don't need to be indebted to you or your brother because of my situation."

"Are you always this stubborn?"

"Yes."

What am I doing considering taking her to my house? At least there I can protect her. I don't know what I'm doing bringing Lexi over to my house. She clearly wants nothing to do with me, but at least there I can protect her. I know Jaxson said things have been progressing fast with Dakota, and she may be spending the night at his place. If that's the case, I'd hate to see Lexi alone. Out of the blue Lexi questions, "So if you drive a Range Rover, like I do, why doesn't your brother have any parts around his shop to fix it?"

"You drive a Range Rover? He does have some parts to it, but since I have not had any issues with mine, he really hasn't had a need to keep them stocked."

I am trying to gauge her reaction to the ranch and the house when we pull up, but she just looks straight ahead. Her eyes did get big for a moment, but she didn't say anything. Oh, but how I wanted her to say something.

"It's beautiful" she says finally.

SHE SPEAKS!!!"Well, thanks." I wink. I notice her blush a little, but she looks down at her hands sitting clasped in her lap. I feel my pulse race. It's been so long since I've even gone on a real date – let alone bring a girl back go my place. Her quiet judgement of the ranch left me amazed. Most women gape at the large property, and automatically make assumptions about my income. Assumptions that are more important to them than who I am as a person. I smile gently and explain, "My parents built it . . ."My parents built it, and Jaxson and I made renovations to it after they were killed," I say this as nonchalantly as possible. I don't want to alarm Lexi or cause her to pity me. I notice her eyes flash over to look at me, but I continue, "It was hard. WE kept the integrity of the home, but changed the design. We still feel our parents all over this ranch.""I can't imagine losing my parents," she says softly. Her eyes are trying to search mind, but I put my head down. She continues with her thought. "I still need them so much."

"Yeah," I sigh. "It was tough in the beginning, but luckily I had my brother to help out and we had friends from the community. It wasn't like we were orphaned at age two."

Still, it wasn't right for them both to be gone.

CHAPTER SEVENTEEN

LEXI

We pull up outside of a giant, wrought iron arched gate with letters intertwined spelling out JBR. Royce stops and punchs in a code and the wrought iron gates open and we drive through. As we drive under the arched gate I am in awe, but I am trying to hide it. I need to act as if this is a daily occurrence in my life. No need to look too shocked and make both of us uncomfortable.

Even in the dark, anyone could tell this is a huge working ranch, with over five hundred acres and multiple buildings and barns. I assume some of these barns are for the horses, but others must be home for other animals.

There is the biggest greenhouse I have ever seen, and beyond that there are fields and fields of crops planted from what I assume to be the starters from the greenhouse. As we go up the dusty driveway, my mouth keeps getting wider and wider, and my eyes are huge and bugging out of my head.

"Um, not wanting to sound stupid but what does the 'J' stand for in the ranch name?"

With a huge smile on his face he turns to me and says, "The 'J' stands for James, as in Royce and Jaxson James."

"Oh well, I guess you don't just work here, do you?" I laugh. "Yeah, you're right. I don't just work here. I do work here, but it's more than just day to day chores on the ranch. If you didn't figure it out yet, my brother and I own it. I have the bigger share of the farm, since he has his garage. I have a share in his garage as well, but it is only a small share, like twenty-five percent.""By the looks of this place, I'd say you were rich," I blurt out. Blushing, I put my face down. Did I just actually say that? It's true, though. I've seen houses like these before on TV, and they go for over a million dollars by themselves, but with so many on this beautiful land, it must be worth a fortune. "But that doesn't matter if you are." Because it seems to be a concern of Royce's about people using him for his money. place is the most amazing sight I have ever seen. I stand in amazement, my mouth hanging open when reaching the main house. I have never seen anything like it. This house is a gorgeous log cabin home, with five bedrooms, and five and a half bathrooms. It is made for entertaining. It is a party planner's dreams come true with this amazing background.

As we walk through the front door, Royce was explaining as he shows me around his incredible home. From the front door we went down the hall and on the left is the dining room, with a masculine chandelier, and across the hall is a half bath, decorated in shades of grays and blues. We stroll deeper into the house there is a great room and bar area. The gourmet kitchen has stainless steel appliances and pure granite counter tops. There is a wraparound porch and a sun room, and we took the stairs and we saw his in-home office he keeps it tuck away about half way up, this is not to distract any from the house.

On the second floor, there are four bedrooms each with

their own walk in closet, each room also has their own bath room. On the third floor, there is another office, a gym, and a movie and gaming area. The last guest room is up-stairs on the third floor with the last bathroom as well. If the entire house wasn't enough for one person there is a four-car garage to top it all off. I wonder what his bedroom looks like.

"Cat got your tongue?" Royce asks. "No, not at all. I am trying to take in the amazingness of this place that is called a home. I take it this is your house – the part that you own? Here I am drooling over it like an idiot," I giggle.

"You have not looked like an idiot, but yes I do live here. Let's get you something to eat. You've had a very long day."

"Don't go out of your way for me, just a simple salad or Pb&j is all I need." I stats. I don't want him to think I am any more pitiful than I feel. I mean I have to worry about my weight and now my pocketbook. I should just have Royce take me back to the inn and forget I exists.

"I am sorry but this establishment does not do simple. If I take the time to cook, I am going to enjoy everything that is put into my body. How about I make us some quick steaks and potatoes?" Royce asks.

"Sounds good but I don't want you to go out of your way for me."

CHAPTER EIGHTEEN

ROYCE

L exi, why don't we head towards the kitchen and I will get dinner started?"

"Sounds good, but really you don't need to go to all the trouble of making steaks at this hour."

"Are you always this stubborn? How about you just sit down and relax. Would you like something to drink. ? Do you like beer or Mikes Hard Lemonade?"

"You already asked if I was that stubborn, and I would love a Mikes, please. Strawberry lemonade is my favorite. I could sure use it after the few-run-ins I've hadwith Justin today. I am still wondering why I ever dated that man. Calling him a man is being too generous."

"If it is any conciliation, I don't believe any of what I overheard him yelling at you. I think you are." I get tongue tied; I never get tongue tied around women. I am always confident, and I have the life to prove it.

"You were saying, Royce?" she asks blushing. I am sure she wants to know where my mind was going with that thought.

I can feel my own cheeks turning red. "I was saying, he is wrong and you shouldn't be ashamed of your body."

"Thank you..."

We fall silent, neither one of us knowing what to say.

Throughout dinner and the tour of the house, I could feel the wheels in her head spinning. I have a feeling she is trying to put two and two together. Jaxson is right, she is smart, and I might not be able to keep our secret for much longer.

"Royce this house just keeps getting better and better, but I have to know, why did you make it so big if it was just going to be you living here?"

"Well, umm. . . That is a very good question, Thought I stumbled over my words, I did appreciate her blunt questions. Lexi didn't play games, I could see that and it was a refreshing change from the girls I'm used to. She seems to say what is on her mind, even if it makes the rest of us uncomfortable. I know I could say I always saw myself in a bi house with a wife or children, but would she believe me? Doubtful. It sounds like a terrible line to win her over. I could say I wanted a party house, but that's a lie. I don't want to lie to Lexi.

I finally settle on my answer. "I have always lived in a more than modest house and this is a way for me to keep in touch with my parents. As for the rest of the answer, I don't know I get up and walk to the stove where I have the steaks frying in a pan. "Come on, I am starving and you must be hungry as well. We need to go get some food." I change the subject.

As soon as I mention she must be hungry, she clams up and looks down and starts intertwining her fingers together. I lean over and grab her hands and pry them apart. She looks up at me.

"I told you not to act that way around me, Lexi. I think you are beautiful just the way you are. You should not agree with anyone who says negative things about you. Not even yourself."

CHAPTER NINETEEN

LEXI

I come to the conclusion Royce is a great person. There were only a couple instances where the conversation lulled. Usually after he gave me a compliment, which was my own fault. I tend not to believe people, I am so used to only getting a complement when I was expected to spread my legs. This is comfortable, and it's odd because I hardly know him, but I feel so calm sitting by him. I really just want to taste his lips. They looked so soft and willing to be kissed. Down girl, I chastise myself, you just met the man this afternoon. You can't go jumping into the sack with him. It must have been a long time since I had any form of booze because this Mikes Hard Lemonade is hitting me hard.

"Um Royce, is there any way I can get a taxi? I think I need to head back to the inn. I must have been more tired than I thought. I am sorry."

Lexi don't worry about it. I can take you back or. . ."

"Or what Royce?"

"Or if you want, I have plenty of room here if you want to sleep in one of the guest rooms. I don't like the idea of you going back to the inn and running into that jackass again. Especially when I am not around to protect you."

"Thanks Royce, but I didn't bring any clothes with me and I don't want to intrude on your space or routine."

"Will you stop it! It is not a hassle, and you won't intrude on my space. I will call the inn and make sure Dakota knows where you are. Plus the way Jaxson and Dakota were with each other, they are probably still out talking or even back at his place on the other side of this property. I know for a fact he was taking her home and cooking her dinner like I am trying to do for you. Would you like me to call or text him to see if he took her back to the inn?"

"Um that sounds great. You can text him. I don't want them to be bothered by us."

"So, there is an us then?" Royce says wiggling his eye brows. "Wait, what? We hardly know each other. We're barely acquaintances." I notice his eyes flicker down and his body posture sink a bit, so I quickly continue, "But I suppose given all that we've shared together in the few hours, we're definitely in friend territory." "Oh, wow. You're not subtle with your friend-zoning, are you?" I giggle. "You said it. Not me." He shakes his head and looks at me as if he is inspecting a piece of art. "You have a beautiful smile." My heart stops and I'm filled with butterflies I long since forgot existed, but their wings are quickly torn apart by the monsters hiding in my heart. "You really don't want me, Royce. The things Justin said are true. You heard him – I'm no good. I suck at sex. I know that's lame to admit, but it's only fair. Might as well be honest and not waste anyone else's time. No man is going to want a girl like me."I feel defeat wash over me. I just want to go bed and hide under the blankets until I can get my car. I have a feeling that isn't going to happen. "First of all," Royce states authoratively, "You are a woman. Not a girl. I already told you, I don't believe a thing just said."I flinch at the power in his voice, even though he is only saying kind words. As if noticing this he gently rests his hand on my shoulder. "You're tired, Lexi You need to eat and get some rest. It's not good to go to bed on an empty stomach. Let me help with that." "Fine I give. I am hungry and shouldn't be drinking this on an empty stomach, because my head is already fuzzy. I am not a big drinker."After the wonderful meal Royce made for us, I find myself stifling a yawn. My eyes are heavy, and I know I am more than ready to sleep off this endless day.

"Well I probably should be heading back to the inn," I announce.

CHAPTER TWENTY

ROYCE

I don't think that is going to happen. I can set you up in one of my guests' rooms. We can discuss this all tomorrow morning after a good night's sleep."

"I can't stay here. All of my stuff is back at the inn," Lexi whines. "You don't think I can handle myself? I'll have you know I've been doing just fine before you came along.""It's not that. I just don't want you around that guy. He seems dangerous – and he's in the same building as you. It's not safe."

"You planned this behind my back?" Lexi yells.

"No... not really. Dakota didn't want to be near Justin and she didn't want you alone with him in the same building."

Does she not see how much danger she is in? Justin is nothing but bad news. How can she not see this? I am definitely putting in more security.

"Lexi, either way you were going to end up here or I was going to be staying in Dakota's bed while she is with my brother. None of us are taking any chances."She stands there, breathing heavily and looks at me as if she is either going to kiss me or punch me. I'm not sure which, and I'm pretty sure she'd gives up figuring it out herself when she storms off down the hallway.

Lexi storms off down the hallway. She passes the bathroom and walks into the only other door on the left. My bedroom. The door slams shut. It looks like I am going to be sleeping in a different room. What a feisty woman! I am definitely not letting her go no matter how hard she tries to pull away from me. I know she's the type of girl that'd give me hell and heaven – she has no shame in expressing herself and her raw honesty is refreshing. I'd never have to guess where I stand with her. I'd always know. That is, if I could stand with her at all.

After Lexi storms off to my room. I make my way to the guest room at the other end of the house. I sure hope I can get some sleep tonight.

CHAPTER TWENTY-ONE

LEXI

In my haste to get away from Royce, I stormed off down the hallway and passed the bathroom. I walked into the next door I came to. . . his bedroom. It has to be. This is the only room he didn't show me during the tour of his house.

I pace back and forth in Royce's personal bedroom, knowing that I am acting like a little child who was sent to her room without her favorite toy. Justin is still trying to run my life by just being in the same town I am in. Why can't he move along and find another girl. I know I shouldn't be taking this out on Royce but he is the one who won't give me the space to process. I know Dakota is worried and having me stay here smells like something she would plan depending on how well their date went.

Oh, man, now, I have to figure out how am I going to stay in this room all night? I wish I was going to be cuddling up next to his hard body. I catch myself dreaming about what he wore to bed and how his body would feel next to mine.

After changing into a pair of shorts and a tee shirt, I climb into Royce's bed, hoping my mind will turn off so I could get some sleep.

After about two hours of laying there staring at the ceiling, I figure sleep is not going to happen. I get out of bed and grab my notebook out of my purse. At least I can brain storm some ideas. I also grab my phone to see if Dakota has texted me.

D: Hope you're not too mad at me. I think this is for the best.

Me: I was when I found out. I stormed off and ended up in Royce's room. I am sleeping in his bed. Well I am lying in his bed. Wishing he was in here with me. Sleep isn't happening. I am brainstorming ideas right now.

D: Get some sleep. It has been a long day.

Me: Not happening. Talk to you in the morning.

D: Night.

CHAPTER TWENTY-TWO

ROYCE

Four o'clock comes fast. Normally I am not up this early, but I couldn't sleep and decided to start the day. I left a note on the door to the master bedroom to let Lexi know I will be out in the barns and when I will be back in.

I need to get my chores done early. I want to be able to spend some time with Lexi and figure out this whole Justin situation. Is it a coincidence that they're both here? I mean, he is her ex-boyfriend – what's up with that? Regardless of whether he had anything to do with her car breaking down, he is harassing her and suddenly has an interest in doing business with me again. It makes no sense. I walk out the onto the front porch to enjoy my cup of coffee like I do every other morning. Something about this morning is off. I notice right away that I'm not hearing the horses neighing for their hay. As I look closely at the barn nearest the house, I notice the door appears to be ajar. It's a good thing I packed my 9mm hand gun my ankle this morning.

As I start walking towards the barn, my head rancher Willie notices me and walks over to me.

"Hey Royce. What are you doing out here so early?"

"Couldn't sleep. I thought I would start early, but I noticed the doors on the barn were ajar when I was on the porch."

"Yeah I noticed that myself. I am glad there are two of us. I don't want anyone to get hurt."

"Yeah that is for sure. I got extra protection strapped to my ankle. Do you have yours that you carry in case of coyotes?"

"Yeah never leave home without it, Willie replies."

"Good. I hope we won't have to use it."

Willie and I walk towards the barn trying to be as quiet as our boots will allow. I know something is off, but I cannot put my finger on it.

We enter the barn and the horses are eating. What the hell? Who was out here to feed them? I make a rash decision and pull the horses off the hay so we can test it. I am not letting anything happen to these horses.

The hay ends up being fine, so we let the horses back at it. Why would anyone come in here and do the chores? Nothing is making sense to me. Time to step up the security.

"Thanks for the help, Willie. I will check in with you later today to see where we are in regards to the progress on all the projects that need to get done today."

I head back to the house and notice Lexi sitting on the front porch drinking a cup of coffee. She is one of the most beautiful women I have ever seen, and she doesn't see it. The only other person who was more beautiful was my mother. I miss her and my dad everyday. So as I walk closer to the house and she finally sees me she blushes. Like she might have been caught doing something wrong.

"Morning Lexi. How did you sleep last night?" I inquire.

"I slept really well. Thank you. I am sorry I took your room though that was not very nice of me." She says sheepishly.

"It's no big deal. You had a long and very stressful day yesterday and a lot of things were coming at you. I am just happy I could help." Hopefully that calms her mind because I really don't want her to be stressed. I want to take it all away and protect her.

CHAPTER TWENTY-THREE

LEXI

I wake up and walk out of Royce's room into the hallway. I notice he has taped a note to the bedroom door. Went out to the barn to check on things. I will be back by 11am. There is some coffee, fruit, and bagels in the kitchen. Help yourself.

I get up, take a quick shower, and braid my hair. I throw on a pair of jeans and a t-shirt then head towards the kitchen in search of coffee.

After pouring my coffee and toasting my bagel I head out to the front porch to enjoy my breakfast. I'm lost in thought as I sip on my coffee. This trip has been a huge disaster. My car breaks down and running into Justin makes that two strikes. One more strike and I am out of the game. What else could go wrong? How in the hell did he find me here? He had to have been following us. I mean, I don't entirely known if he came here for me, but it feels like he's haunting me. It fills my stomach with a sick emptiness. Why can't he just leave me alone, and find a different female to torment?

Maybe someone from the debate team wants him long term. According to him, I am not that special, so why is he stalking me? I can't prove any of it. I can prove that he is talking me, but why would he spend all this time in a small town that holds nothing else for him? Whatever is going on here, I can't handle it. All I want to do is live my life and make my business a huge success. I never wanted to get stuck in this town. We're falling behind on our business plans, and now I have to deal with the stress of Justin again. Dakota and I have worked too hard to have all of this fail. I have to get things figured out and fast. I just want to live my life, and make my business a huge success. Dakota and I have worked too hard to have it fail.

I look up as I take a drink of my coffee and notice Royce walking towards the house.

"I see you found the coffee and bagels," Royce states.

"Yes I did. Thank you. I am heading in for a refill. Would you like me to pour you a cup?"

Royce follows me into the kitchen, and he leans against the counter as I pour the coffees.

"Are you sure you slept well" Royce questions?

"Okay, I thought I would be able to fall asleep since I was so tired, but I stayed awake and worked for a little while. You caught me. I thought I kept the noise down, I am sorry."

"Well, I was thinking last night. Since I don't want you near that jackass, your not sleeping that great, you said so yourself, and we don't know how long he is staying, you will stay here at the ranch with me. As you can tell, I have plenty of room, so consider your argument a moot point and just say 'Yes Royce, I will stay with you in your home, until my car is fixed.'"

CHAPTER TWENTY-FOUR

ROYCE

WHAT! I can't move in here. Extra rooms or not, this is not my house I hardly know you and I already paid for the room at the inn. Anyway, I will be fine I have Dakota, and we have things we need to get organized for the big party we are throwing in Chicago. We do have a business to run as well," Lexi argues.

Oh, my goodness! This girl is about as stubborn as they come. Granted I may be overstepping my boundary, but we both know its safer here at my place and certainly more comfortable. Why is she fighting this so hard?

"Fine, she will stay here as well. Oh, and Lexi that is final," I said with a wink.

"You can wink at me all you like, but I am putting my foot down. You have already done too much."

I smile, "Oh, it is final because I know everyone in this town and just because you paid already doesn't mean you can't get a refund."

"Royce, this is not your fight. I have handled this guy

for four years and he is going to get bored and leave me be."

"No, I don't think you're right about this, Lexi. I think he is going to try and make your life a living hell."

"What's more hellish than laying there and practically being raped for the last four years," Lexi yells while waving her hands hopelessly.

When Lexi tells me this I about lose it. This is going to be coming to an end. I don't care what I must do, but Lexi is never going to have to feel that way again. I protect what is mine and Lexi doesn't know it yet but she is becoming mine. I am not letting her go, I need to protect her. I have never felt such as strong urge to protect and love someone so fierce. I wonder if mom is giving me the push from beyond the grave. I know she will not steer me wrong. Thanks for the help mom, I am going to need all the help I can get with Lexi's stubbornness.

"Even more reason for you to stay on the ranch," Royce argue.

"Look Royce, I haven't talked to Dakota since I texted her last night, I am going to go call her and see how her date went. You know do the best friend thing. I will be back down in a few minutes." Lexi changes the subject.

"Well, if you'd like, when you get done with you phone call, we will go grab an early lunch."

Lexi doesn't answer me as she turns and walks out of the kitchen.

CHAPTER TWENTY-FIVE

LEXI

I head upstairs to call Dakota. As I approach Royce's room I hear my phone ringing.

Sitting down on the bed, I answer. "Hello."

"Hey Lexi! How are things?" Dakota asks, laughing.

"Laugh all you want. How did your date go last night?"

" Jaxson is great, Lexi. I could see myself falling for him. I think I already am."

"Please D, tell me you didn't sleep with him."

There is a pause, "D," Lexi question, exasperated. Still silence.

"You did sleep with him!" Lexi exclaim.

"I am so not sorry that I did either."

"As long as you're happy. I just don't want to see you get hurt. What is going to happen when we leave here and head to Chicago?" I ask.

Lexi, I don't have everything figured out, but things are going to work out."

"I am glad one of us thinks so. Right now, I am not so

sure," I sigh. I haven't told you what happened last night after you left with Jaxson, before Royce showed up." I take a deep breath before I continue with my story.

"I had a missed call from my mom so I stepped outside to call her back. She was worried and I was filling her in on all the major drama. Anyway, after I finished my call, I was in my own world. I accidentally ran into someone and it happened to be. . ."

"Oh, no Lexi don't tell me it was Justin," Dakota says.

"Okay I won't but I would be lying. As I was saying we had a loud lengthy yelling match in the middle of the street right in front of the inn; long story short, he knows that I know about the debate team, but he doesn't know that I have a video of it. Speaking of which why am I keeping the video?"

"You're keeping it so if Justin does anything you have the upper hand. Like if he tries to blackmail you or does anything wrong then you will have something he can't deny. "Oh before I forget Royce has all but demanded we move into his spare rooms while my car is being fixed.""Honestly, Lexi, I think he's right. Justin lurking about the inn gives me the creeps. I think I'll stay at Jaxson's though"

"Wait who are you and what have you done with my best friend, Dakota?You can't leave me alone with a stranger!"

"I am still me. I just feel that maybe Justin is a little out of our league when it comes to his craziness. I also got the same lecture from Jaxson, so this isn't a total surprise to me."

"And to make matters worse, I just blurted out to Royce about being practically raped for the last four years. I don't know how I can go back downstairs and face him."

I need to get all of this Justin stuff out of my mind and determine if I can trust Royce. I mean he has had the opportuinty to force himself on me. He hasn't though, so maybe I can trust him on the surface, he doesn't send my creep radar off but then again maybe my radar is off since Justin's creepiness didn't register either. For now he gets surface trust. He must her the rest of my trust.

" Oh my gosh, sweetie. You didn't . . ."

"I did, but he was going on and on about Justin trying to make my life a living hell and it just kind of came out. Look, I don't want these two men making choices for us. They just met us," I explain. Exasperated, I continue. "I can make my own choices!"

"Look Lexi, I know this isn't the way we had planned for this trip to go, but maybe we should let Jaxson and Royce be our knights in shining armor. I have to go for now, but I will check in with you later."

"Bye. Dakota," I say, hanging up the phone.

I push the off button on my phone and throw it down on the bed. I sit there with my head in my hands. I can't believe everything that is happening. Its only been a little over two weeks that Justin walks out, and probably thinking I can't live without him, My brand new graduation car is tampered with, being stuck in a town and having Justin be here as well, and always being in the same place always a step ahead. Then if everything isn't enough I am going to throw my feelings for Royce on top of all that.

He is one very good looking man, he is being overbearing and protective. But I don't want him to make all my choices for me. This is my life and I need to live it.

CHAPTER TWENTY-SIX

ROYCE

I start walking up the stairs in search of Lexi. She has been gone for a long time, and I want to make sure she is okay. I am rounding the corner at the top of the stairs when I hear her scream, "I can make my own choices!"

I am not sure what this is all about. I stop in the doorway of my bedroom and find Lexi sitting on the bed with her head in her hands. I walk over to her. "Hey is everything okay?"

Lexi looks up, "Dakota agrees with you and Jaxson. Apparently, I am going to be staying with you while she stays with Jaxson."

Look, Jaxson's house is on the back of the property. It's about twenty or so acres. You will not be that far away from each other. We have internet and a great chef, namely me, who will cook you anything your heart desires."

"Royce, are you trying to flirt with me?"Oh, man. She sounds genuinely curious. How can she not know what flirting looks like? I wouldn't do this for just anyone – she's got to know that. It seems as if all the men in her life have been demeaning or belittling her to the point of nothing. All the men in her life have been demeaning her and belittling her to the point of nothing. She literally doesn't feel like she deserves a great man. This just makes me want to throttle Justin that much more.

"Lexi, I am going to take you back to the inn. Dakota and Jaxson will meet us there. At that point in time, you will gather all of your belongings and then you will stay with me. It is not safe for you otherwise. Honey, you need to take the stress off your shoulders and let me carry some of it for you." I don't know why all of these pet names are coming out so freely and naturally.

"What do you want out of all this? I learned a long time ago that nothing comes free. You are moving me into your house, and what I become your sex slave?" Lexi mocks.

How dare she say that! Oh, I am seeing red at this point. "No, all I want to do is keep you safe and that means you need to be here so I can keep an eye on you and know you are safe. I don't want sex from you. I want to get to know you and maybe become friends first and if we like being friends we might be able to go on a date."

There! I had to knock her down a bit only so she wouldn't have an attitude with me. I know I already want her in my arms and in my bed, but that's not why I'm doing this. I also know that after saying that, I am going to have to work twice as hard, but now I have time I can devote to her and keeping her safe. Tonight I will take her to a bar and have a few drinks and dance. I'll see if Jaxson is willing to bring Dakota along and play my wingman. If I have both of their support, I'll be able to gain Lexi's trust. It's crazy what this girl is doing to me and how much I want her to like me. I haven't been this nervous in a long time. Man, I hope this works.

CHAPTER TWENTY-SEVEN

LEXI

Two hours later, D and I have checked out of our room at the inn. We're back at JBR. The inn keeper was sad to see us go. She is a nice lady, but she knew everyone's business She is a nice lady, but she was always gossiping and getting into everyone's business. I can't count how many times I had to listen to her tell me about a couple from two towns over who rent a room on the weekends. She'd go on and on about how scandalous it was I guess that's something I'll have to get used to.

Woah! Wait. What am I thinking? There is nothing to get used to. I'm only in this small town until my car is fixed. Why am I have thoughts of staying? Is there anything or anyone I would want to stay for? It's too soon. Lexi, I tell myself. Way too soon.

"Penny for your thoughts, Lexi?"

Um. . . . I have been caught. I can't tell him what I am actually thinking because he will think I am a crazy person. I mean, we haven't even kissed or held hands. Sure, he can

72

cook a killer meal, but that isn't everything. It's not as if I can't cook myself a great dinner. I don't need a man to feed me. Of course, I wouldn't mind seeing him standing by a stove in his boxers after we .... Okay, no more! I can't think like this! I hardly know this guy. What is happening to me? "I was just running though my lists in my head. You probably won't see me a lot since I have a lot of work to do. Do you need to have a WI-FI password for the connection in this huge house of yours? I have some business to attend to," I needlessly snap. Why am I acting like a such a witch in heat? He is being nice to me, and here I am, trying to sabotage anything that might come of this.

"Yeah, you can use my office upstairs, no password needed." Royce replies. "I am sorry. ' I say. "You are just trying to be nice to me, and I am just being defensive because truthfully, I don't know of any other way to be. I feel like a worthless piece of scum, and I just want to hide," I sigh. "I have a lot on my mind."

"I am a really good listener if you ever want to get anything off your chest,"Royce suggests.

"I just can't fathom how Justin found me," I confess. "Plus he was the one who left me. He told me I wasn't good enough to be in a family like his. He said and I quote 'Lexi, you are too fat and stupid to be in my family. ' So, after I cried for a long time, Dakota reminded me what he did to me and I was over it. But this shit isn't going to stop, is it?"

"To tell you the truth, I don't know. Therefore, you should stay with me. I can protect you and make sure nothing happens to you."

"You can't protect me forever. I have work I have to do in Chicago. The Chicago event is Dakota's and my first big party we're planning. This party has to be a success. I am hoping my car will be done in time."

CHAPTER TWENTY-EIGHT

ROYCE

I hate that I can't just walk up to Lexi and wrap my arms around her and tell her everything is going to be okay. The thing is, she needs someone to take away her pain. Part of her seems to acknowledge what Justin did to her is wrong, but another part of her acts like she deserved it. It's the part that doesn't accept compliments. It's the part that doesn't trust me and keeps pushing me away. Lexis needs someone to show her how worthy she is.

Lexi needs someone to show her own worth to her. If she thinks she is going to go to Chicago all on her own she has got to be crazy. I will be going with her. That is all there is to it. I know it may seem crazy, but I can't stand seeing her broken. I haven't known Lexi that long but damn do I care about her. Besides, with Justin practically stalking her and potentially messing up her car, I don't think it's safe for her to go alone. Maybe if I give Jaxson a call, he can come too. After all, we know how to handle Justin. These girls don't. Okay, that settles it. I'm going to reach out to Dakota and Jaxson. Dakota will need to be on the same page for this to work. She knows Lexi better than any of us. I'll keep this to myself, though. No need to stress Lexi out. She can stay in the dark just a little bit longer. I pull out my phone to text Jaxson, when I notice Lexi typing away at my office computer. She gets this fierce look of determination when she's focused on something. It's cute. Shaking her head, she whispered to herself. "That's not the right one. We need a different center piece for the tables." Caught up in her beauty, I don't even notice the words coming out of my mouth. "Lexi, go on a date with me. We never did get to have lunch together. Let's go out tonight!"Well, I've never been known for being subtle, I guess. "What?" Lexi asks, clearly startled. "I don't know Royce. It sounds nice and everything but. . ."

"But nothing Lexi. I am taking you out. Be ready at six o'clock for dinner, and whatever else we decide to do." I smirk.

She is blushing when she responds. "Has anyone told you that you are a little domineering? I know you want to protect me, but I don't need another father figure. But, yes, I would like to go out with you." Lexi smiles.

Lexi walks into the bathroom, and I walk out of the bedroom towards the room I had been sleeping in to call Jaxson. I will ask him and Dakota meet us at the bar for drinks and dancing after Lexi and I have dinner.

Please don't be busy. I need to figure out what we are going to do with these girls.

"Hello."

"Hey Jaxs, I need to talk to you. We need to make a plan and keep the girls safe," I bellow into the phone. "Hey, good. Dakota is with me and she seems fine with the change. She hates Justin as much as we do. You wouldn't believe the stories she told me. Poor Lexi has gone through some pretty rough situations."

"That's good since it took an act of congress for Lexi to agree, but she finally agreed and that is all that matters now. Make sure all of the security is on high alert, because we had someone get in last night."

"How did someone get in? But yeah, I will make sure that they are doing above and beyond especially now that the girls are on the ranch." Security never became an issue until the dog breeding incident, and after that we just kept them on to make sure none of our competitors do not get any wild ideas. As it seems you can't get rid of the Kramers so its a good thing we still have the security. Why were they don't doing their jobs last night. Can't worry about that now, Jaxson will take care of it for me.

"I am going to take Lexi out to dinner on a date. I think you and Dakota should meet us at the bar for some drinks and dancing afterwards. I have it bad for her, but she seems oblivious. Bro, it takes all my strength to not grab her and kiss her or even hold her hand. I bet you feel the same way about Dakota with all the time you've been spending together."

"Yeah, I didn't want to say anything because I felt like a pansy. I didn't want my man card taken away. I know Dakota has a lot of issues but, I am willing to work on them with her and go at her speed. That is what you're going to have to do with Lexi. Just go at her speed. We are not like Justin in the least."

As I entered the office my heart stops as my practically stumble into the door frame. I find Lexi super focused at what she is staring at on the computer screen with her forhead scrunched and worry lines have formed. She is so determined, nothing is going to stop her from accomplishing all of her goals. She is going to be successful no matter what gets in her way. She has no clue how gorgeous she is. It's clear other men like Justin have screwed her head up, but now it is my turn to make sure she knows what it's like to truly be loved. She will know how beautiful she is, and if I am lucky at all, maybe one day we can be more than whatever it is we are now. I want forever with her, I am man enough to admit it.

Clearing my throat, I say." You better go and get ready for our outing tonight."

"Oh, my gosh, you scared me to death, Royce."

CHAPTER TWENTY-NINE

LEXI

Walking into the bathroom, I am consumed by my own thoughts. Holy heck! I am going on a date with Royce, and it hopefully will be fabulous. I guess it's time to go pick out my outfit and try to connect with Dakota. I need her to help me pick out said outfit. I've got to look extra good. This is where I find out if there is any potential for us to be more than friends. I can't imagine a guy liking me, especially after all that happened with Justin, but I won't lie – I like the way Royce makes me feel.

Dakota comes over to Royce's house and helpes me pick out my best outfit. It can either be casual or I can dress it up. I pick a white sundress which hits me right above the knee. It also shows off my cleavage a little more than I normally would. I pair it with a jean jacket, fun earrings and a necklace. I got to love my five-dollar jewelry lady for this combo, because it is killer. Since it is still chilly in the evenings, I decide against the sandals that I usually pair with this outfit and put on my brown ballet flats.

I also grab my spring time Dooney and Bourke satchel purse. It is big enough to hold everything but still lets me to feel feminine. It's also not so huge that it takes away from my total appearance. Then to top it off, my Maui Jim sunglasses to pull everything together. I put on some lip gloss and mascara, and I straighten my shoulder length hair so it is soft. I imagine him running his fingers through my hair. Things may be moving way too fast with Royce, but it feels right. He feels right. After all this pain, I think maybe I've found something happy. I hope Royce likes what he sees tonight. I have to be honest, I am trying to go for the good night kiss. I do not want to end up as just one of the guys. He said it was a date, I just need to stop over thinking everything.

I walk down the stairs to meet Royce at the front door. He turns and watches me walk down the last few steps. I feel like a princess the way he is watching me. It's such a foreign emotion. For so long I've been abused in every way you can imagine. This is a pleasant change, and as much as I want to doubt Royce's intentions, he just seems to perfect. Everything seems so perfect right now. I almost fall down the stairs, because the way he is looking at me takes my breath away. I am smiling to wide that my cheeks were hurting. He is in a pair of nice tight wrangler jeans with a black button down shirt, sleeves rolled up to the elbow. To top off his appearance, he has on his black Stetson hat, rodeo buckle, and black boots with spurs on the back. They're the kind only for show not the ones that you wear when in rodeos.

"You look fantastic." Royce acknowledges.

"Thank you. You look great as well. Shall we head out?" I counter.

"Yes we shall. We have a reservation for seven o'clock tonight, and it will take about forty-five minutes to get there." Royce announces.

The next thing I know, Royce grabs my hand and leads me to his truck, opens my door, and helps me in. My head is spinning. This is a check in the no-just-friend's category.

I have never had anyone do that for me. After he gets in the car we head out of the ranch. His hand never leaves the top of mine. My stomach has so many butterflies in it I don't think I will be able to eat anything. Soft music is playing in the background as we chat and continue to get to know each other.

As we continue chatting, I am getting more and more nervous. I am so very aware of everything that is coming out of my mouth, because I do not want to slip and delve into my past.

"Umm since I am stranded with you," I say smiling "I am in need of a good doctor, can you help me with that? I just need to refill a couple of prescriptions and I am out of refills." That got his attention. I can see the wheels spinning, he also wants to let me know that he knows that he has seen my birth control pills.

"I didn't notice you taking anything other than your birth control pills, what are these other pills for and are you okay?"Do I let him stir or do I just explain it to him. Hmmm. I think I will let him stew for a minute or two. He is getting agitated more out of worry it looks like, anyway it looks like my fun just ended. "I have a little depression issue that is taken care of with a medication, plus I have what is known as Hypothyroidism. In a nut shell its hard for me to stay slim, I have dry skin, usually cold, and can loose my hair easily. There are other issues with it but that is also taken care of with medicine and every so often I have to get my blood drawn to make sure my dosage is correct. I have a serious form of it and it has been hard to pinpoint the correct dosage. So, if you can help me find a primary doctor who could refer me to an endocrinologist would be great." I say with a smile.

"Let me make a few calls and see if we can get you in tomorrow." He says.

"I appreciate that. I know that there is a time and place for that and it is not on the first date."

"It is not an issue, I feel like we are past the first date formalities because of how we met and all the talking we have done." Royce says. I realize any man who might want to marry me will need to know. Whoa, Lexi! Who said anything about marriage? You are getting ahead of myself again. Well now maybe I can take a breather. There is too much going in my mind. I need to figure out how to get through it all. Maybe I should talk to someone but who? I don't want to put this on Dakota, she knows my issues and normally she supports me but this is different. I just don't want to stress her out. I think she had a worse start in life than I did and its not fair to put my crap on her. I know friends can handle anything but I feel like I need to do this alone. I think Royce is starting to notice I am in my own world.

When the next song comes on the radio it helps bring me out of my deep thinking. I don't want Royce to notice that I was off in "La La Land." The song is catchy and I wanted to know who sang it.

"Royce do you know who sings this song? It kind of sounds like my life story."

"Oh this is the song is called "Take It out on Me" by Florida Georgia Line. They are a fairly new band in the last year or so."

"It seems like a good song, but do you know what it means?"

"Well, I think it means that if you're in a bad relationship, or just out of a bad relationship, then there will always be one friend whether it be male or female that will listen to you and not judge you. I also think the literal meaning could be that you can take all your frustration out on that person, whether it be sexual frustration or platonic frustration." Royce says.

"That is a cool way of looking at it, but from listening to the actual words. It could also be a cheating song." I say.

"I guess but there are always two sides to every story."

By this point I have to change the topic, so I decide to talk about his belt buckle and what that means.

"So Royce, were you in the rodeo?"

"Yeah, I used to bronc ride and was decent, well, at least I held my own. My brother and I also team roped," he tells me.

"Why did you give it up? I mean, I know I am a prodding into your personal life. If you don't want to answer, it's okay too."

"Naw, its fine. We just got tired of traveling and wanted to put down our roots. It's not like we got hurt or anything. Every time the rodeo comes to town we consider entering,but usually we stay in the stands these days."

"I wouldn't mind watching you ride, granted I would be would be a nervous wreck hoping you wouldn't get hurt but that is besides the point." I say with a chuckle. "Why don't you talk about your parents?" I fell bad the moment I ask, but it just came out of my mouth before I could think about it.

"They were in a car accident about ten years ago. I still miss them, though."

"I am sorry. I didn't mean to pry, but sometimes my mouth knows no filter and stuff just spills out of it before I can stop it."

I fell terrible. I don't want him to be sad. I was only curious, but curiosity did kill a cat, so my mouth needed to behave.

CHAPTER THIRTY

ROYCE

I watch Lexi walk down the stairs and my breath completely leaves me. I am speechless. She is wearing a simple outfit, but the way she is carrying herself, just screams sex kitten. What did I get myself into tonight? I put my hand on the small of Lexi's back to lead her out the door. Man, this is going to be a long night. In a good way, though.

"I will help you up into the truck," I offer.

"Thanks. This dress seems shorter now, and I don't want to flash anyone." Lexi blushes.

How much of her body flushes red or a very nice pink color when she blushes? Stop thinking like that, man! She may not want more out of this. She might only want friendship. After some light chit chat, Lexi asks me about my parents. I hope I don't offend her when I don't go into very much detail. I want this night to be perfect.

Olive Garden was the fanciest place I could get into on short notice. I hope she actually eats. She needs to eat. Luckily, I know we won't have to wait when we get there since I put a call into the manager and normally they do not do reservations, but money talks. Granted I hate throwing money out like that, because I am not my money, I am a regular guy who works hard who happens to have more money than I know what to do with. I also don't want to be in a crowded area. I want to be able to sit and talk and not worry about who is going to hear and who is going to see us. I am not ashamed of her, but I want to be able to get to know her without any distractions. It will be nice to have her in a relaxed setting without her always looking over her shoulder.

As we enter the dining establishment, I walk straight up to the hostess and tell her my name. A spark of recognition flashes in her eyes. Instead of saying the wait time she says. "Right this way, sir."

"Royce, how did we get seated so fast?"

"Lexi, I just called ahead and they put my name on the list ahead of time. It was no big deal really."

"I have never heard of Olive Garden taking reservations or putting names on the list early. Why do I feel like I am not getting the full story here?"

"There is no story, really. I eat here a lot and I know some of the staff. It's no big deal. Sometimes they might put my name on the list, so when I come in I don't have to wait too long."

"I don't think that is the full story," Lexi gives me the side eye and continues saying, "but this is nice, and I am having a wonderful time. Thanks for bringing me out tonight. I can't wait to meet up with Jaxson and Dakota for drinks and some dancing!"

"Yeah, I think it will be fun. I haven't been out dancing in a long time. Well, normally I don't dance, but it's nice to kick back and relax with a drink after a hard day of work."

"Agreed. Everything looks so good."

"Have you decided what you want to eat? I can give you

some recommendations on my favorites if you need help." I say.

"No, I am okay. I am thinking I might only want the soup and salad combo, with a raspberry lemonade."

"Really, that is all you want?" I ask her. Damn her! I know what she is doing. She barely even looked at the menu before answering. Her voice is still quiet and she has a distant look in her eyes when she stands up. In a gentle voice, Lexi says, "If you will excuse me, I am going to the little ladies' room. If the server comes back before me, will you please just get the soup and salad combo. That one," she points to the Zuppa soup on the menu. "I can never pronounce it correctly." She smiles sweetly as a blush creeps up from her neck to her cheeks. Sure, but I am not ordering you that. You will get pasta just like me with the soup of your choice and you can have some of my salad if you want.

"I can do that for you." I smile at her.

Being the gentleman I was raised to be, I stand as she rises to go to the ladies' room. I am still looking over the menu, well pretending to look since I know what I am getting, when our server comes, and asks if we are ready to order. I put the drinks, appetizer, and our main courses order in at the same time, but I ask them to space each order out so we have time between courses. I don't know about anyone else, but I hate whenthe orders seem to come out at the same time or out of order.

CHAPTER THIRTY-ONE

LEXI

Right after I walk into the restroom, the hair on the back of my neck stands up and I have chills running down my spine. I immediately walk back out and looked around. Hm, interesting. I don't see Justin or anyone who looks like him. I hurry and finish in the restroom and head toward our table. On the walk back to my table I glance over to the bar. That's when I see him. Justing is sitting at the end of the bar smiling and waving at me. I took a stutter step and that gave him enough time to make lewd and rude gesture that my dress was too short.

I feel all the blood drain from my face. It's as if I am standing outside of myself, but at the same time I am very much aware of my body because it's shivering. I've never felt this cold. I've never been good at masking my emotions, so of course the moment I sit down Royce reaches for my hand.

" What is wrong?" He asks gently, rubbing my thumb with his.

I can't tell him. I just shake my head as if to say, everything is alright. I change the subject with a smile. "Did you order?"

"I did. The drinks should be here in just a few minutes."

CHAPTER THIRTY-TWO

ROYCE

When we were seated, I made sure to sit facing the door so I can see who walking toward us. These events with Justin have me a bit on edge. I notice Lexi making her way back to the table. Her posture is different. She doesn't seem as relaxed as when she left. What the heck happened in the five minutes she was gone? I groan inwardly, because I know there is only one thing that can make her go from carefree and loving to white as a ghost. How in the hell did he find us here?

I'm being ridiculous. I am not going to jump to conclusions. I have no idea what happened while she was in the ladies' room. Maybe she received a stressful text about work? Or maybe she's just nervous about this date. Whatever it is, she will have to tell me. I am going to ask her, but until then I will assume nothing is going on. Hopefully she will tell me what happened, and if it is Justin, I can protect her. As she sits back down, I ask, "How was the ladies' room?" She flashes me a confused look, and I laugh at myself. Well, that was smooth. She musters up a small smile. "Fine." We both know it wasn't fine at all. This is going to be harder than I thought.

"Alexus, honey, you are white as a ghost. What happened while you were gone? I know something happened, and I can't help you if I don't know what's going on," I use her full given name instead of Lexi, I have started doing when I wasn't throwing her off her game with using Baby Girl or any other pet name. I love the way honey and baby girl just slip off my tongue just so naturally. She slips her hand from mine. Taking a deep breath she begins. "I saw him. I mean, I saw Justin. He was sitting at the bar as I walked by." She pauses. There's so much pain in her eyes. She thinks no one sees it, because she avoids making direct eye contact when talking about him, but it's there. "He smiled and waved at me. It's not a big deal. Can I just sit here with you and forget that I saw him? He also showed me my dress was short and I might not have the body for it. It is not a big deal. I just want to sit here with you and forget that I saw him."

"Oh, Lexi, honey, I am sorry you ran into him, but trust me, he cannot get to you. He knows it too. Because of that he is trying to enter your mind and put doubts about everything. I don't want him to ruin our night, but maybe we should do something else."

"No, I want to go out with your brother and my best friend tonight after dinner."

As soon as she says that, our appetizers come out. I ordered cheese sticks and calamari with sauce. By the look of her eyes she didn't expect it.

"Hope you don't mind, but these two are my favorite. I wasn't sure you would like the calamari, so I ordered the cheese sticks as well."

"I love both. I am surprised you got so much. Thank you. It looks so good."

We continue talking and getting to know each other. There have been many openings where I can tell her about how rich my family is, but I think Jaxson and I need to tell the girls at the same time. I know we need to tell them, but it is not the right time.

I am not ashamed of the money we have, and I really don't think that Lexi and Dakota would think different about Jaxson and I, but once that is out, you really can't take it back. I am pretty sure Lexi is not a money grubbing women. She is has never asked for anything and she already thinks I am rich. She just doesn't know the extent of it.

Next order that comes out is the salad and her Zuppa soup. Since I instructed that there is only to be one plate with the salad, she has a weird look on her face.

"Dig in," I tell her, she is eating her soup so extremely lady like. She isn't spilling or slurping it. She is even and using her bread stick to slosh up some of the juice. She is eating in such a way that it doesn't dribble down her chin. I have never seen anyone eat like they were having dinner with royalty. I don't normally dine with my social circle. I have never fit in.

I ask her, "Do you want some of my salad? We would need to share this plate, since I guess they forgot yours."

"No, thank you. I will be okay. I will ask for another plate when they bring your pasta out, Lexi states quietly.

We continue our conversation without any awkward silences. It seems as if I could never run out of things to tell Alexus. I have endless questions about her family and her sister who she isn't that close to, but she takes it in stride. She is clearly waiting for the time when she can repay me with all these questions that she has in her head. I am sure she has many questions about me, but I make sure not to keep the subject on her life. Now is not the time to explain my history. We need to deal with Justin first and then Jaxson and I will tell the girls about our wealth. See, the whole town knows how much we boys are worth, but it's never been a big deal. It's not like we go around flaunting our money or acting like we're famous. We help where we can by contributing to our community.

Of course, we have had our fair share of gold diggers. It's usually people who are new in town, or people who came here to specifically meet us. That's why we've had to keep this from the girls. After getting to know Lexi, I know she's not like those other girls. Those other girls would eagerly accept a nice dinner – and still ask for more.

The next course comes out and it's the main event. Two big heaping bowls of pasta,one with Alfredo sauce and one with marinara sauce. I didn't know which kind she would like. They bring us plates so we can split and do half and half.

I hear a timid and weary voice ask me, "Royce, where is my salad?"

"You need to eat a good meal and not just rabbit food and a soup."

"But-"

"No buts. Now please just eat, no arguments. We are having a fun and relaxing evening."She takes a deep breath and rolls her eyes. I look at her, offering up my most flirtatious grin that's been known to win over the most stubborn of women. She giggles. "Oh, okay. Fine. It seems you have selected my favorites again. Would you mind if we split the two dishes?"

"I would love it if we split the dishes. Now, eat up."

She just smiles a shyly smile at me. The rest of dinner goes off without a hitch. She keeps thanking me repeatedly, and I just brush it off as if it si nothing, because in reality it is nothing. Of course, she doesn't know that. It is in this very moment that I know I want this woman for the rest of my life. I am in awe of her. Her genuine kindness and the way she smiles at me. Looking at her, it's as if I see my future. It sounds crazy, because I haven't known her very long, but suddenly she has become such a central focus of my life. I catch myself making a mental note to take care of her. It'd be great of Jaxson feels the same way about Dakota. I don't imagine Lexi would even try to stick around if Dakota leaves. She is going to be taken care of.

I have Lexi wait for me on the front benches in the front of the restaurant while I go to the restroom. I do not want her waiting in the car by herself.

As soon as I enter the restroom, I see him. What is the guy doing and why is he waiting for me? He needs to get a life.

"Justin are you following me because I told you no?"

"Nope, the way I see it you owe me since I sent that bitch to you."

"You need to stop right there. You are not welcome in this town or the whole state of Montana. As soon as I place a call, you are going to wish you had never set foot here again. I suggest you get back on your side of the continent."

"You will regret this for the rest of your life," Justin sneers.

"No, actually I think I am going to be fine and have a happy life."

As I am leaving the restroom, I send a quick coded text to Jaxson about my run in with Justin, suggesting him to be on high alert tonight.

"Ready to head out?" I ask Lexi.

"Yep, I am so ready for a couple of drinks and dancing."

"Sounds good." Man, I wish I could tell her about the run-in, but she is finally settling back down. I take her hand and the leftovers, and we head to the Range Rover.

CHAPTER THIRTY-THREE

LEXI

After a wonderful dinner, Royce pays the check. While we are walking, he sits me down on the bench just inside the doors to the restaurant while he uses the restroom. When he returns, we are walking out the front door when I hear from behind me, "Hey bitch, don't think you will ever get away from me." It's the voice of yours truly. Royce grabs my hand and leads me out of the restaurant, quickly getting me into the car. Before Royce gets the door shut I have to get in a few quick shots.

"What do you want from me, Justin? Seriously just leave me alone and go find a different girl to harass! I am tired of it, and you just need to get on with your life. You know, the one without me in it. Don't you remember you are the one who left me!" I scream.

"You don't get it, do you? I own you. I ruined you. I have marked my territory, and guess what? You are it. You belong to me even if we aren't dating anymore." Justin states coldly.

"You do not own me. No one owns me except me." I say my voice starting to shake. Istop talking, and wait for Royce to get into the car. I want to get out of there and away from Justin.

At this point, I cannot control myself. I start to cry, even though I don't want to cry in front of Royce, especially since we are on a date. I just wanted to have fun. I thought Royce and I turned a corner.

"Lexi, please don't cry. We will get through this together. Now please tell me, do you want to head back to the ranch and finish the date there?" Royce asks.

"No, we will not get through this together, because guess what? We are not together, we barely know each other, and we just met. This is our first date and it is being ruined," I cried. "I do not want to go back to the ranch. I am not going to let him ruin our night. He is probably going to follow us where ever we go. I want to spend my night with you, Dakota, and Jaxson. I want to be dancing the night away." I have tears running down my face by this point. I feel like such a fool, but I'm not giving into Justin. I will never let him control me like that.

CHAPTER THIRTY-FOUR

ROYCE

After our run in with Justin, I figured Lexi would want to go back to the haven of the ranch, but she didn't. I honestly don't know how I am going to keep her safe while we are out in a bar. I'm glad I got a text off to Jaxson when I did.

Once I saw Justin wasn't going to let things die down in the parking lot, I did the only thing I could. I wrapped my arms around Lexi and let her cry on my shoulder. She felt so good in my arms. I am not going to lose her. I am not blaming her for breaking down there's no way anyone could be calm cool and collected while having someone harass them around every corner. The fact that she doesn't think it involves both of us, well she is wrong because I don't care that we just met literally yesterday afternoon, She is mine and I will protect her. I just have to gain her trust.

As we drive to the bar to meet up with Dakota and Jaxson, I grab her hand to let her know I am here for her. It is truly amazing what a simple touch can do to help ease the pain for someone. I am happy my touch puts some color back in her cheeks. Pale is not a good look on her, but, every great man knows not to say anything in a situation like this. I need to come up with a master plan, but first I am going to cherish the rest of tonight. Maybe Dakota, Jaxson, and I can start working on one. Granted, for parts of the plan, we have to keep Dakota out of the details. It would reveal our wealth and I don't want Lexi worrying about that right now. Justin is a much bigger problem than my bank account balance.

When we arrived at the local bar, Jaxson and Dakota are standing by Jaxson's parked truck waiting for us. Dakota runs up to Lexi's door and swings it open. She pulls Lexi out of the car and wraps her into a bear hug. Jaxson walks to my side of the truck.

"Hey bro, what is the plan for tonight?" Jaxson questions.

"I think we should not let on to either of the girls about the dangers. You and I will need to be extra aware of what is going on around us."

"Sounds like a plan."

"Remember we need to act as normal as possible. Do you have your piece on you? I have mine," I explain.

"Yeah in my boot," Jaxson replies.

The four of us walk into the bar. I do one clean sweep of the parking lot and don't see Justin or his car, but I have no doubt he will be here at some point tonight. I stop and talk to the head bouncer when we walk past the door. I need as many people on my side if anything happens tonight. It doesn't hurt that the bouncer, Bryce is a good friend of mine. Jaxson continues to walk with the girls to the table in the back corner of the bar, where we have designated our table.

"Hey Bryce, I may have a situation here tonight. Did you see the girl I walked in here with?" Bryce nods. I continue, "She has an ex-boyfriend who has been stalking her. He has already shown up when we had dinner. He and I exchanged words. I wanted to let you know Jaxson and I both have weapons on us. You know that will be a last resort, but I wanted to let you know the situation. He drives a red Porsche."

"I will keep my eyes out."

"Thanks man," I give Bryce a brotherly smack on the back as I walk past him to join the rest of the group.

The four of us are sitting around the table, Jaxson and I are nursing club soda's while the girls are drinking strawberry daiquiri's. We both need to keep our heads clear in case Justin showed up. Sam Hunt's song "Raised On It" starts blaring through the speakers and Lexi jumps up. "I. Love. This. Song. Dance with me, Royce!"

"Sure thing Lexi."

We walk to the dance floor where I am in awe of how she moves. She throws her arms up and she sways with the music. I know I must look like I am ogling her, but I don't care. I am mesmerized by her.

CHAPTER THIRTY-FIVE

LEXI

I know Royce said he doesn't normally dance, but I couldn't help but pull him out to the dance floor with me. I love this song! I know I am not a very good dancer, but I don't care I am going to let loose tonight and enjoy myself. I have this hot guy with me. I am ready to party! Justin who?

After the song ends, we navigate our way back to our table. I pick my drink up from the table and take a long, slow swallow from it. Liquid courage. I stood with one should pressed into to the wall listening to the music. Royce walks up behind me, puts his arms around my middle, and nudges me back slightly against him. I have always secretly envied women whose men hold them like this. It feels so good. I am glad I have my drink in my hands or I wouldn't know what to do with my hands. I should touch him, but I have never had a man want me to touch them before.

As the song "H. O. L. Y" starts to play by Florida Georgia

Line, Royce reaches up and takes my drink out of my hands and pulls me against him closer. At this point I am touching him and can feel his erection. Be cool Lexi, don't overreact! You don't want to blow this. Oh, I can't get over how wonderful his arms feel around me. His strong arms, I could get lost in them. It would not take much for me to fall even more for Royce than I already have. He has been nothing but kind and understanding since I met him. In return I have been nothing but a spoiled, broken witch to him. I truly do not know what he sees in me, but I see the spark in his eye when we talk toward each other. Why has someone not snatched him up already? As the song comes to a close, Royce leans in and nuzzles my neck, right below my ear. I need to use the restroom, but I don't want this feeling to end. I don't want to move from this spot. I don't want to lose this feeling. Suddenly Royce spins me around in his arms, leans in and lightly touches his lips to mine. Like a crazed animal, I tighten my grip on his neck and start kissing him back. I am totally taking the lead here. After a brief shock, Royce deepens the kiss. I don't know how long we stood there, it couldn't have been more than a few minutes, but to me time stood still. Yes, our first kiss!Royce is the first to break the kiss. No. No. No. He puts his for forehead to mine and quickly kisses my cheek.

"Royce, I need to use the little girls' room, I will be right back."

"Don't you think you should get Dakota to go with you?"

"The bathroom is less than 10 feet away and I haven't seen anything that should be of concern. You can see the door from right here. Just stand here and wait for me."

CHAPTER THIRTY-SIX

ROYCE

As I watched Lexi walk into the bathroom, I can't help but be overwhelmed with this feeling of uneasiness. None of us have seen Justin since we left the restaurant, but I can't shake this feeling that something bad is going to happen. I know there is an entrance in the back of the bar by the manager's office. There's a small chance Justin could have slipped in that way. I decide to walk up to the women's restroom to make sure Lexi is okay. I need to know she's fine. I knock on the door before opening it and shout, "Lexi, you doing okay in there?"

I have to know she is okay.

"Royce! Oh my gosh! Shut. The. Door. Right now!," Lexi yells.

"I'm sorry. Well, not really, I had to know you were okay."

"Royce, I will be right out."

I should stand right here by the door, but I will respect Lexi's wishes and go stand by our table and wait for her.

I stay there and wait for ten minutes before I can't stand it any longer. As I walk up to the bathroom I can hear a commotion coming from the back hallway. Lexi... I take off sprinting towards the sound.

I reach Lexi and who I thought would be Justin, but it isn't, I bellow, "You let her go right now!"

"Sorry man, I have a debt I need to pay," the mystery man snarls.

The mystery man has stripped Lexi of her jacket and is dragging her by the arm. I can see tears streaming down her face. Her eyes are filled with fear mixed with anger. Lexi tries to fight and yank her arm away from this guy, but he only latches on tighter. "You are not getting away from me, so stop fighting me," the man sneers.

I yank my phone out of my pocket with my left hand while I grab my gun with my right. I need Jaxson's help and fast. I don't see a gun, which is good for me, but that doesn't mean the man doesn't have one. When Jaxson answers his phone, I bark." Back door now!" No other words are needed.

By the time Jaxson and Dakota reach the back door the man managed to pull Lexi through the door into the chilly night air. I instantly see goose bumps on her arms. I don't want to spook Lexi or this crazy psycho who is trying to kidnap her, so I hold my gun below my waist and angle my body in front of it.

"Oh my gosh... Steve," I hear Dakota yell from behind me.

Hearing Dakota yell this guy's name scares him enough that his step falters and Lexi can release herself from his grasp. She runs past me straight into Dakota's arms. Her tears immediately start to flow.

As much as I want to comfort and protect Lexi I know she needs her best friend right at this moment. Jaxson runs past both of the girls stopping at my side. I have my gun drawn on Steve so he isn't about to move. He is standing there shaking. "What do you think we should do with him, bro?" Jaxson questions.

"Personally I think we should tape his ankles and his wrists and leave him here. I know Justin is behind this. He won't be too far behind to see what happened."

"Good plan. Let me grab the duct tape out of my truck."

After stripping Steve down to his boxers and socks we taped Steve's ankles and his wrists and sit him down on the concrete. We leave him in the back alley of the club. The four of us walk back into the bar and out the front doors. I stop and tell Bryce about the attempted kidnapping, suggesting he should call the police.

I walk out to where our vehicles are parked and find Dakota and Lexi sitting in the back seat of Jaxson's truck. "Why don't you take the girls to my house and wait for me there? I am going to stop at the store and grab something sweet for all of us. We need to come up with a plan. What happened tonight is out of the ordinary for Justin. Bringing someone else in, he likes the game too much."

"I hear you loud and clear."I hear Dakota yell out the open car door, "We love red velvet cake. It our favorite!" I can see the fear in her eyes, but she's acting like nothing is happening. I know why. It's the same reason I'm playing it cool, for Lexi's sake. If we show our fear, she'll know just how much danger she may be in, and it will only upset her.

"Make sure to stop at the security station and give them a heads up. I will see you in a bit."I know Jaxson hears me when he nods his head and climbs in his truck. I turn to walk around the front of my truck so I can go and pick up a red velvet cake. I hop into my own truck and start the engine. Taking a deep breath, I brace myself for what's to come. I know picking up cake is the last thing I should be doing, but I need to clear my head first. I need to figure out what exactly is happening here and how to take care of it.

CHAPTER THIRTY-SEVEN

LEXI

After everything that happened with Steve in the back alley, all I want to do is go back home and crawl into bed. Wait! What? That's not home ... The thought came into my head so naturally, there's no denying that I feel at home on that ranch with Royce. Crazy as it may be, being with him is the closest I've felt to home in a long time.

Jaxson drives both Dakota and myself back to Royce's house. Jaxson announces that Royce will be back in twenty minutes after he picks up our dessert. Red velvet cake! A man after my own heart!Suddenly, I'm hit with a crushing realization of what has happened. A guy tried to abduct me! And why the heck did Royce and Jaxson just tie him up? Why didn't they call the police themselves? My skin crawls as I remember Steven's words. He has a debt to pay. For who? In my heart, I know the answer, but I don't want to think about. Instead, I tell myself Justin can't really be that dangerous and that I'm just being paranoid.

Maybe I heard that guy wrong. Maybe not involving law enforcement is just how this town rolls. Jaxson pulls into the security shack on the outskirts of their property and talks in code to the guys standing there. I am only half listening. I am mentally and physically exhausted, but for cake I can manage a little longer.

Royce shows up in his living room about fifteen minutes after we arrived. He strolls in and sits down on the couch right next to me. "I brought sweets," Royce announces with a soft laugh. "Lexi, I know it's hard to talk about and we could just ask Dakota, but I would really like it if you'd share with us yourself what exactly happened between you and Justin. I know a little, but I need to know more. We both want to keep you guys safe, so we need to know what we're dealing with here."

Lexi picks up a cupcake from the plastic package and sits back against the couch. "Here is the short version: we dated for almost four years, I found out he had been cheating on me for pretty much our entire relationship with some of the girls on the female debate team. They taped him, but he didn't know about it until the fight in the middle of the road yesterday. We never spent a whole lot of time together. If it was only the two of us, he would always be playing video games or texting on his phone. He was always telling me I would look prettier if I would lose some weight, and he would taunt me with food, mainly sweets. He broke up with me the week before we were to graduate. I don't know why he is stalking me, but I personally think it is to keep tabs on me to ensure that I fail. Finally, on the rare times he did want to have sex with me he would force himself on me and say to me. Tell me how you like it."Aside from choking up a few times, I finished my story relatively fast. I needed to. Talking about it was hard, but if I knew if I got it out fast enough, it'd be over. I take the smallest bit out of my cupcake, so I have something to do other than look at Royce or the others. The whole room fell silent once I stopped babbling like an idiot. I don't know what Royce expected to hear, but I'm guessing it wasn't this. Finally I look up and see the see such a pure fury in the face of Royce and Jaxson. No one wants to be the first one to talk. I sit there and finish my cupcake. I can't feel sorry myself anymore, and I don't want anyone else to either. I have to move on, and I am picking this very moment to start. I stood up and announced,I stand up a break the silence. "I am going to go upstairs and go to bed. I'll see you all in the morning." No one says a word when I leave. As I'm walking up the stairs, I remember I haven't moved my stuff out Royce's bedroom. I'll have to put that on my to do list and take care of it first thing in the morning

CHAPTER THIRTY-EIGHT

ROYCE

After everything Lexi has told us, I am stunned. Who would stoop so low to stalk an ex-girlfriend just so he could keep tabs on them? That is out of character even for Justin. From what I remember people tend to disappear if and when things ended. We have in the past after my parents died come to the ranch and try to sabotage either the animals food or the animals themselves. With the Kramers being who they are I expect in the near future that Lexi is going to be target of a bad accident or flat out murder. The reason Jaxson and I don't talk about our parents death is because we suspect that their accident wasn't an accident at all, but there is no proof. That is how the Kramers work. Jaxson and I decided we need to keep both girls safe and not let them out of our sights. We still aren't going to say anything to either of them about our financial resources or the fact that we know the vile things Justin is capable of. But our bank statements are not important.

I go upstairs to check on Lexi, and I find her curled up in a ball laying on my bed. She has changed into a t-shirt and a pair of sweats. I stroll over to her and try and wake her up. I figure she probably didn't mean to fall asleep and would like to take a shower before bed. She needs to wash the events of the night off so she could start fresh tomorrow. "Lexi, honey why don't you wake up and take a shower? It will help you sleep better."

I walk over and scoop her up off the bed. I carry her to the bathroom and let get ready for her shower. Hell, I am going to get in with her I need to hold her. She looks so fragile right now. It isn't about sex with Lexi it is showing her I want her more than her body. Yes, there is a sexual undertone but nothing will cross the line. I will never do anything to take advantage of her, unlike that douche bag Justin. He clearly took any opportunity to get into her pants, and it sounded more like rape than two consenting adults having sex. He took any opportunity to try and get into her pants. It sounded more like rape than two adults having consensual sex.

"Lexi, honey why don't you get into the shower? You'll feel better." I say again. This time I get an answer from her. "I don't have the strength, Royce. I feel so weak both physically and emotionally. I am trying to be brave and make it look like I have all my stuff together, but this is really starting to be too much for me handle."

"Okay, don't worry about it, I will help you but first I need to go get rid of our guests. I will be right back to help you."

There is something about Lexi I can't put my finger on. Before I can help her I have to be a good host and tell my brother and Dakota, goodnight and we will regroup later.

I quickly walk back downstairs to where Jaxson and Dakota are sitting. "Hey, Lexi isn't doing that great and I think we need to have a meeting when shes working to get a game plan together. Is that okay with everyone?"

"Yes" they both say in unison.

O. K. we should probably meet at about ten O'clock tomorrow in the morning. She is usually up in the second office trying to get everything together for the trip to Chicago." I pause because I am not sure how this is going to come across. "Lexi can't know about this planning meeting. She is in no shape to handle it."

Dakota gasps because she is surprised by my statement but, then I see her reluctantly nod in agreement.

"I have a couple meetings that I need to go to in the morning but they should be done by nine-thirty. I can make it by ten or just a little after." Jaxon explains.

If we are all agreed, this needs to stop. Right now, I need to get back to Lexi. Jaxson keep Dakota safe. I know Lexi is worried about her as well, but she can't keep doing this to herself. She is about to make herself sick."I look over to Dakota who is yawning. She's just as exhausted as the rest of us. "Don't worry bro I am on it. I will see you tomorrow. We have Ranch business to talk about before this big meeting about Lexi." Jaxson says, and I know what he means. It is the car and the fact that the girls are not going alone on this trip of theirs to Chicago. I don't care if it is a new company, they have a maniac on their hands and he must be stopped.

I walk my brother and Dakota to the door and wait with the door open until they are both safely in the truck before I close the door. I lean back on the door thinking about the fight I am going to have on my hands when Lexi finds out her plans are about to change. She is a planner just like I am. She doesn't like surprises or a sudden change in plans – and that's all she's been experiencing the last few days. I can handle it, though. Let the games begin. I finally make it back to Lexi. She seems to be okay, but her eyelids are half open as she yawns. She is leaning gently against the wall of the shower, as if she is too exhausted to support herself. She doesn't notice until I wrap my arms around her and bring her to me. She jumps and starts to fight me. "It's okay," I whisper "Lexi, it's just me, honey. I'm sorry. I should have told you I was coming in. I should have asked ...""No," she says softly. "It's okay. I want you here."

It is sad really, but I know she doesn't want my pity. I'm not going to give her any. None of this was her fault. She didn't ask for any of this. The only thing she wants to do is get on with her life. I would love that to include me.

"Come on Lexi, let me take you to bed. I want to hold you. Don't worry you are safe with me."

"Thank you Royce"

After helping Lexi into bed, I climb in behind her and hold her. I hold her while she fell asleep. Tonight, is the first night I feel at peace. I feel my mother and father and know they would be proud of not only me, but Jaxson as well. They know we will be okay now that, we have found love.

The next morning I was just hanging up the phone from making the appointment with Dr. Baxton when Jaxson shows up the next morning, and we choose to use our wealth for good. We are going to take the girls to Chicago via our private jet, the one we use for our business travels. I plan on booking two suites at the hotel next to the location of the event they are coordinating. Jaxson decided that we would hold off telling Lexi and Dakota that we own the jet. I am perfectly fine with that plan. Our cover story is going to be we are borrowing the plane from a former business associate because traveling privately is safer than commercial. Yes, we are filthy rich. . . no we don't flaunt it.

"Okay, so we are in a hundred percent agreement that we will use the jet and you are booking the hotel as soon as we are done here, am I correct on that?" I repeat to Jaxson.

"Yeah, plus we are not backing down. We are going with them to keep them safe. Don't forget to book extra security for the event. They can throw a fit all they want. This is happening, it is either this or they don't go." Jaxson states.

"Yeah, I know. I am happy we are both on the same page with this plan. If one of us didn't want to do it, it would be a lot harder, but I have to tell you, last night was the first time in a long time that I felt at peace after Mom and Dad died. I don't know what it is about her, but man. I think mom and dad sent Lexi and Dakota to us. Do you feel that way with Dakota?""Man, I'm glad you said that. I wasn't going to admit it, but that's exactly how I feel. The first night I held Dakota in my arms, I knew I couldn't let her go. Mom and Dad definitely have been looking out for us. Dakota coming into my life, so suddenly and at just the right moment, it's all the proof I need. Things have been moving so fast, but I'm grateful for that. I needed this. I needed her. Is someone sick, why do you need an appointment with Doc Baxton?"

"No its not me, it is Lexi, she was telling me how she needed a doctor for some refills for some prescriptions. She says its nothing major, but I already just want the best of everything for her. Then it is settled. We cannot let them get away from us. No matter how much push back we get from them."

Dakota walks into the room and cuts me off, "Let, who get away?"

Oh, good grief! I am glad she was not here two minutes ago. Think, think, think. I lie. "Oh we had a couple of people wanting to use our stud services and it will be a financial benefit both parties involved."

"Oh, that is good. I'm happy to hear business is going well for you guys. I hope our business will be as profitable one day."

"It will, it takes time. From the work ethic I have seen you and Lexi show, you will be bigger than any celebrity party planner out there."Jaxson declares.

"Guys we have a colossal problem. It doesn't matter what precautions we take, Justin is going to find Lexi everywhere she goes through the find your friends app on her phone."

"We will buy her a new phone. Problem solved," Jaxson chimes in.

"You can buy her a phone, but good luck getting her to accept it."

"Stop guys, the cell phone is the least of our worries. How are we going to keep Lexi busy? I don't want her to leave the ranch unattended. Even if someone goes with her, we should be very careful. He is obviously not opposed to walking up to her in broad daylight. It doesn't matter who she is with. He wants her to be mentally non-functioning. I saw pure evil in his eyes. He is out for blood. I don't know what he is capable of doing, but we need to be extra careful and have security with us always. I don't want that prick anywhere near her," I say.

"Who is going to tell Lexi that she has to stay on the ranch unless she has a chaperon? Because I have known her a long time, no one ever tells her what to do or how to do something. She is very head strong. She is not going to give up her independence no matter if her safety is in danger or not," Dakota informs.

Dakota has a point. Lexi has fought me on everything. I only want to protect her. Why can't she see this? She is one stubborn woman!

"It will be fine. I think she is too busy to want to leave with everything that has to get done before we leave in a week and a half. Oh, by the way, both of us are going with you two and I don't want to hear any complaints. Please, Dakota. You get to tell Lexi that one." I say smugly.

"Oh wait a minute! I didn't sign on for this, you guys are changing the plans? How are we supposed to get there? Are we still staying at the same place? What if Justin shows up? These are things we need to avoid," Dakota says panicked.

Jaxson reaches for Dakota's arm to soothe her. Holy crap! How does he do that? She was going to hyperventilate, but with his mere touch she calmed down. I want things to be like that for Lexi and I.

"Baby, shhhh it is going to be fine. Royce and I have a plan. All you have to do is tell Lexi we are cashing in a favor. No, you will not be staying in the same hotel. Everything is under control, we only want you girls to be safe. It will be easy, but you need to be semi forceful with her. It is this way or no way. Got it," Jaxson asks, making sure to stress all the important areas of our plan.

"Yeah baby I got it." Dakota answers.

Once they leave, I go in search of Lexi. Guess its time to break the news to her.

"Hey, Lexi do you have a minute? I have a couple of things to talk to you about."

"Sure, I am almost done here anyway. What's up?"

"Well I was able to get a hold of Dr. Baxton, he can get you in today. We are going to have to leave in a half an hour to get there on time."

"Okay and how do you know Dr. Baxton?" I ask. I am worried that this is going to be a special favor for Royce. Part of me is thinking he is over reacting.

"Dr. Baxton is and has been our family doctor since my grandma and grandfather built this house. Well its not the exact same as when they were alive but kept it in the family. Don't worry this is the best in town. I would not take you to some half rate doctor."

"Did you have to pull any favors to get me an appointment today?"

He is smiling at me like I am ridiculous but I know him. "No, Dr. Baxton only works for our family and at the hospital. His shift is over in a half hour and we are going to meet him in his office at the hospital."

"You guys all go see Dr. Baxton but he only works at the hospital and then on call for you guys? How is that even possible?"

"I don't know that is how its always been. He is general medicine but he likes the fast pace of trauma specialist in the emergency room. This guy does it all. He even delivers babies when needed."

"Well thank you for sharing Dr. Baxton with me. So what did you tell him I needed to be seen for?"

"I thought you could probably use a full physical along with your blood tests."

"Yeah I guess your right its been a couple of years. When I went home for a break and then they just gave me enough refills to last until right about now. Thanks for doing this for me."

"Your welcome now come on we need to go so we are not late."

"Okay what about the other thing that you wanted to talk to me about?"

"Oh, about that well, I don't want you to leave the ranch without either security with you, or myself and Jaxson." I put a smile on the end hoping that it will take the edge off of what I just announced.

CHAPTER THIRTY-NINE

LEXI

"Wait what?!"

"Your safety means a lot to me. This is the best way I know how to keep you safe. Dakota is also going to be chained to Jaxson. It's not just you." Royce told me.

"I don't want to be a burden to you. I just want to stay away from Justin."

As we climb into the truck to head to my appointment I think Royce just wants to keep me talking so I am not going to retreat, but guess what I am multi-talented. I can listen to him ramble on about safety and I can doubt myself and even kissing him at at the bar.

Royce continues with his spiel, "your not a burden, it's a safety thing. I need you safe and I know I can do that here the best. Oh, and also I think now is a good time to tell you that you need to think of us as a couple now. Which I guess is a good thing since you have the appointment. I get to go too."

"Just because you are calling us a couple do I have to

like the pet names you use? Plus, your going to wait in the waiting room right?"

"I can if you want me to, its what makes you feel comfortable."

"Umm let me think on that, I guess it depends on how I feel when the doctor calls me back. I am not very comfortable with doctors, I don't know why I just have never had a good reaction with them."

CHAPTER FORTY

ROYCE

I could tell she was nervous, but this was the best doctor in the united states, I wasn't going to tell her that though. I was going to get the best of everything for her. She deserves it. So its time to get her mind of everything.

"Oh look we are here." I inform her.

"Oh that wasn't a very long drive, I thought I would have had more time to prepare myself."

He whole demeanor just changed and not in a good way. I understand not knowing a doctor but I have a feeling it is the fact that he is on call to our family along with being in the trauma surgeon. I don't even know his official title and it really doesn't matter to me as long as he knows what he is doing.

"Don't worry, baby girl. You will be fine. You yourself said that this is routine. You are going to love this doctor. Just you wait."

"I just don't like doctors especially ones I don't know.

It will be different later on if this is going to become my primary care physician. It is just going to take some time. Promise me you will not leave my side. I don't care if you see me naked, and when they go to do the woman exam I don't want your eyes to leave mine. Got it?"

"Honey, I won't leave you. You will have my hand to hold and my eyes to calm your nerves. The one good thing about Dr. Baxton being our doctor is we don't normally have to wait for test results."

"Huh I never thought about it like that. Okay. I give you permission to ask almost any question you may have."

I wonder why she would say that. She already told me what aliments she has so I doubt I would need to ask anything.

"Okay baby girl. But this is your appointment and I will let you take lead on this and then if I have any questions I will ask. How does that sound?"

"Perfect."

"Oh here we are. I will let them know we are here."

Thankfully we didn't wait long. I could tell that Dr. Baxton changed to make sure he looked nice and not that he just came off of his shift. He wore a white button down shirt and gray slacks. Holding his hand out he shook my hand hello, and then he turned to Lexi.

"Hello, you must be Lexi. Royce has told me a little bit about you and your concerns." Dr. Baxton said professionally.

"Hello, yes I am Lexi it is nice to meet you." She said shyly.

Holy cow she was really nervous. I just squeezed her hand tightly and rubbed my thumb on her hand.

"Why don't you tell me what brings in today."

She started with telling him about her depression and why she struggles with that. She also said she was having issues with her thyroid and needed a refill or even a different dosage. Lexi was very knowledgeable about everything and then she finished with how she needed her yearly exam so she could refill her birth control. She went into her background health and family history of what she knew.

"Okay so lets start with the annual exam, then we can get your blood drawn and go from there. Royce why don't you and I step out for a minute so Lexi can get into a gown." The doctor said to us.

I saw Lexi get a scared look on her face and I knew what I had to do. "Doc, I think I am going to stay with Lexi, she gets really nervous around new people and she needs my support right now." I heard her exhale so loudly. I could see that Dr. Baxton understood my predicament. He left the room briefly before I called him back in so we could start this exam. I did exactly what I told her I would. I didn't let go of her hand and looked in her eyes. I had her curled up into me as much as I could why the exam was taking place. It seemed to take forever but it was finally done. I looked at her and saw her visibly relax, I just smiled at her. The only thing left was doing her blood test. As soon as he took her blood and left to go to the lab, he told us that she could get dressed and that he would be back as soon as he had the test results so we could talk about her course of medication.

"I am so glad that is done with. I hate having that test done. I always feel like I am violated, but I know its a necessary evil." Lexi explained.

"You did good baby girl. Real good. I am proud of you."

To me if felt like we were waiting forever. We were both in our own worlds, you would have thought that we were getting a huge news announcement but nope just regular test results. I was playing on my phone while she was reading a book on her phone. I was starting to get worried because it was taking so long. Dr. Baxton never took this long. Just when I was about to climb the walls when he came back in.

"Okay guys sorry that took so long but there were a few bumps along the way."

Lexi straighten up real fast. "Bumps what kind of bumps." She asked.

"Well I can't give you a refill on your birth control. The dosage of medicine for your thyroid seems to be doing its job, and I am lessening the dosage on the anti depressant." Dr. Baxton spits out.

"Wait back up for a second, I am still on the why can't you refill my birth control. I could careless about the other prescriptions."

"It seems that you are pregnant."

"No, no there is no way I can be. We were always careful. I always took my pill and, and, and, and.... Royce and I haven't even had sex yet, there is no way that I am pregnant."

"Lexi, baby sit down before you fall."

"Lets grab an ultrasound while you guys are here and we can determine how far along you are."

Dr. Baxton goes and grabs the machine. When he comes back he has a wand looking thing, it looks like a long dildo. He asked Lexi to take her pants and underwear off again. I was a little confused so I asked.

"Hey doc, I thought an ultrasound scanned through the belly, why does she have to get partially naked again."

"Well since she is probably not very far along the uterus is better reached with the internal ultrasound and I can get a more accurate reading of how far along Lexi is."

I mean it sounds reasonable enough, so Lexi takes off her pants and underwear and places the flimsy piece of paper that you drape over your legs. I guess its supposed to give a little bit of privacy while the doctor has his hand up the ho-ha. All the sudden I hear a whooshing sound and a lub-dub sound quite quickly. And I see a black and white snow, and then something that is flashing. Dr. Baxton points to that flashing thing and says that is the baby's heart beat.

"Lexi you look to be about ten weeks along."

"That can't be right. I can't be that far along. I can't be.

I can't be pregnant period. I don't want his baby. My ex practically rape me and degrade me over and over again for four years." Lexi is crying hysterically.

I thank the good doctor and get the name of the one of his colleagues for an obstetrician appointment.

CHAPTER FORTY-ONE

LEXI

Oh holy hell. I can't be pregnant let alone have Justin's baby in me. I will never get rid of him now. He can't know. How in the hell did I not known I missed a period let alone two. I guess it was all the stress of the last few months. I just want to be left alone. I just want to go home and soak in the bath. I don't want to tell Jaxson or Dakota yet. Lets just get through the next couple of weeks. Lots of stuff can happen. Dr. Baxton was handing me pamphlets about the first twelve weeks of pregnancy. Apparently my body could reject the fetus. Its a little miracle with it lasting through the surgery and the knife wounds.

"Hey Royce, I don't want to tell Jaxson and Dakota just yet. I need to wrap my head around all the information that we just thrown at us. I just want to go get in the bath and think."

"You need to eat something, and then we will head to the house and how about I hold you for a bit. I don't want to be away from you. We are going to get through this.

Tears are just streaming down my face and I can't stop them. I want them to stop but I can't stop them. How is it that Royce knows the right thing to say to me all the time. I don't deserve him.

"I am really not hungry. I just want to go back to your home."

My world is over. I know it really isn't but it sure does feel like it. I wanted to be over the moon when I found out I was pregnant, I also wanted to be married and the baby to be Royce's. Tears more tears. I don't see them ending any time soon. "Yeah, baby I just want you to know that you are not alone."

"I really wish you would eat something. Why don't we just go through the Taco Bell drive through and that way we can eat later and its still going to be good."

"Okay, but mine will probably just go to waste. I don't foresee me eating anytime soon."

"I don't want to say your eating for two now, so you need to eat. I know this isn't what we were expecting but you and I are going to take care of this child."

"I don't expect you to help me take care of this child, we aren't even officially together. We don't love each other." Man that hurt to say that. I have loved this man from day one. It is too soon to say anything. "I get what your saying I really do but I am just so overwhelmed that I just want to shut down. I have been trying to wrap my head around this situation but nothing is computing."

Royce was very quiet, I figured he would add his two cents. He never stops the conversation right in the middle. I turn a little bit in my seat so I can face Royce and not just glance at him using my peripheral vision. His face is a mask, and his eye brows are pinched together in the middle of his forehead.

"Royce what is wrong?" No answer. "Damn it Royce what is wrong? Please answer me. Don't keep secrete from me please. We both have too much stress with this baby announcement and dealing with Justin and Steve."

He finally mumbles, I have to really listen to make sure I get everything. He says "they are behind us. I want to try and loose them but I don't like the look I see in Justin's eyes via my mirrors, that is how close he is. One 'break check' and he will hit us."

"What are we going to do?"

"Lexi, I don't know what we are going to do. That seems to be the million dollar question. I know what I want to do but I need to be smart about it."

"I just want to be done living in fear. Can we just talk about something else? I don't care if they are still behind us."

"What do you want to talk about? I am all for a distraction right about now. What did you have in mind?"

"I don't know." I say with a sigh.

"Well, Lexi there is something that I want to talk to you about. I know you just said that we aren't in love and that it is too soon. Well let me tell you something. I am in love with you. So Honey, hold on tight because I think my parents brought you and Dakota to Jaxson and I."

"You love me? That is not possible. No one loves me, my own parents didn't love me."

"Don't talk about yourself like that. You got me baby and I am not letting go. I don't care that we just met a few days ago. I know this is fast but I know its right."

All of a sudden Royce goes quiet again, and the winkled forehead was back in full force, then I heard the tall tell signs of a car speeding up.

"Royce what's happening." But before he could answer my question, our car is propelled forward with the help of someone pushing on it. "What the heck is going on?" Again my question goes unanswered because he is trying to hard to keep our car on the road. It is getting more difficult to maintain. Then there was nothing. How could this happen so fast and then it just stops. I go to take a deep breath, as I start to let it out, I am jolted again. Instead of it coming from behind, we are now being sideswiped. Many thoughts are flying through my head and the only thing that sticks is good thing Range Rovers are stable cars and are hard to flip. I see Royce is trying really hard to get away from all this. I want to yell at him to stop swerving and that I am going to be sick. Just as I am about to open my mouth we are hit again and I don't know how it happened but we were hit so hard and it had to have been timed just right to where as Royce is swerving to get away that Justin clipped us at the right time and now we are flipped over. But Justin doesn't stop their. He continues to ram into us. At this point we are sitting ducks. I feel my seat belt tightening around me. It is really uncomfortable. I want to take it off but I don't dare, I don't want to get hurt.

"Baby girl, are you okay?" I hear Royce ask me so quietly that I am unsure if it was real. I want to answer him I really do but I can't formulate any words. As soon as I start to say anything I open my mouth and a scream is all that comes out. Is it a scared scream, a worried scream, or a hurt scream. I don't know what kind of scream it is because I am all those things. How am I going to get this information to Royce. I know he needs to know but I think he is also hurt. How am I going to help Royce. He needs me.

"Royce are you okay?" I finally get out. I am still in so much pain but I need to make sure he is okay.

CHAPTER FORTY-TWO

ROYCE

What in the world is going on. I can't believe this guy. I am coming to the conclusion he is never going to leave us alone. So he hit us, he hit our car more than once. I was swerving to try and get away and then next thing I know he must have hit us just right to make sure we flip. We landed on our side and we are still being pushed down the road. Where is everyone, we are in the middle of town and not one person saw this or is watching this? I finally manage to squeak out to Lexi if she is okay, she tries to answer but only her screams come out. It takes a few minutes but finally she manages to ask me if I am okay. I need to answer her, but I glance over and or since the car is passenger side down I look down and see that she is bleeding. It looks like the seat belt is cutting off her circulation. I see blood coming from her but I don't know where it is coming from. All I know is I need to get her to the hospital. I also need to get Dr. Baxton back there. I need to get out of this car. I need to get out fast. I need to call my brother and get him down here to get the car. First things first how do I get this car to stop? Apparently a greater power must have heard because all of the sudden the car is stopped and doesn't move any more. I don't hear any other cars, maybe Justin left. Okay time to get my plan into action. First call ambulance, then Jaxson, and finally Dr. Baxton to meet us at the hospital.

"911 whats your emergency?"

"My finance and I have been in a really bad accident and I need ambulance and police." I state as calmly as I can. I can't freak out. I give the operator on the all of the information and she says that they will be there in a few minutes. I thank her and tell her I need to call for a tow and my personal doctor to meet us at the hospital. Reluctantly she lets me go to make the calls. I know I should probably call Jaxson first but I decide to call Dr. Baxton just to make sure he is able to be there.

"Dr. Baxton, is there anyway you can meet Lexi and I back at the hospital?"

"Why do you need to go to the hospital you just left here twenty minutes ago?"

"We were just hit by a vengeful ex of Lexi's and he is very adamant that he needs to kill her and me in the process since I won't let her leave my sight."

"Okay, I am still at the hospital do you know when you guys are coming in? Also it would be very helpful if you can tell me some of the potential injuries."

"Well we are waiting on ambulance so I am hoping to be there within the next half hour. The car is on its side. The side in which Lexi is on if you get my meaning. Also she is bleeding and I have no clue where its coming from."

"What about yourself? Where are you hurt?" I respond with "my head mainly hurts. I have a huge headache and my arms hurt. I had them locked for the most part trying to keep the car under control. Other than that I probably will just be achy. I am more worried about Lexi. Especially with the news you gave us today about a pregnancy."

"Okay thank you for the heads up I will have the trauma rooms ready when you get here."

"No worries. I don't want anyone else caring for Lexi and myself." Then the line goes dead. I know he has a lot to get ready for us. Okay now for the last call.

"Hey Jaxson, I need you to come get us."

"Why do you need me to come get you? What is wrong with your car?"

"The car is totaled. Lexi is in bad shape and I am just about to go nuts. Justin rammed us and then he hit us at just the right moment to get the car to flip. It landed and skidded on its side for I don't know how many feet."

"Are you guys okay? I will come get the car. Me and my guys will be their shortly. I will just use the tracking info from the car to your location."

"Thanks, I don't know why I didn't think of that. I might be in worse shape than I thought originally. I have the ambulance on the way and I called Dr. Baxton to make sure he would be at the hospital for us."

"Well it seems like your head is clear or clear enough to think to make those three very important calls. Just relax and everything will be just fine. I will handle the car and you won't have to worry. Concentrate on you and Lexi. Dakota and I will be there as soon as we can. Don't make any rash decisions before I get there."

"Sounds good. Oh I think I finally hear the cops and the ambulance. Don't forget to get a copy of the police report. We are going to have to keep a paper trail when it comes to Justin. Man my head really hurts." That was the last coherent thought before I closed my eyes.

CHAPTER FORTY-THREE

JAXSON

"Dakota!" I yell. "Dakota!" I yell again. Finally I get a response.

"What!" she yells back at me.

"Come on sweets, we need to go. Justin strikes again." That is all I got out before she grabs her purse and is sitting in my truck, now waiting on me.

"What happened? What did he do now?" She asks me.

"I don't know we got to go tow the Range Rover to the shop. Royce seems to think its totaled. He and Lexi are going to the hospital to get checked out. I am do not know how much damage is done but Royce was starting to mumble and I think he passed out right before I hung up the phone." Her eyes are so wide. She is scared but we need to be there. They are our family. "Sweets, we need to be strong for them. I will let you cry on me later when we are not around them. Do we have a deal?"

"Yeah." She nods as the tears are rolling down her cheeks.

"Good. I need to call to get the guys going about getting

out here to tow the Range Rover."

Dakota and I pull up to the crash and I am speechless. There are two ambulances and it looks like half a dozen or so cops. I am frantically looking for my brother or Lexi, I need to know where they are. I go up to one of the cops who knows me and he just shakes his head. A head shake what does that mean? I just talked to my brother, he couldn't be dead. Maybe his head shake was Lexi, maybe she didn't make it and then Royce would be beside himself with grief. My mind is screaming what does that head shake mean? I get closer to him and see that there is a lot of blood. But I see Royce being loaded up into one of the ambulances. I scan the area again because I can't see Lexi. It is then that I realize the car is turned up on its side. The side where the passenger sits. It looks like Lexi is trapped. I go over and see if I can help?

"Is there anything I can do to help get her out?" They say they are waiting for the jaws of life. It just so happens that at the correct time one of my tow trucks pulls up.

"Hey guys I can help you out. That two truck has some tools that should be able to help get her out. That way we can get her out quicker. Is there anything else I can do to help?"

They tell me that they have everything under control. I told them what hospital they need to go to. I know I know we only have one but I don't want them to go to the closet one. They need to get to the trauma center. That is where our doctor is and they are waiting for them. They are apprehensive about driving to the trauma center but they do it anyway. I just hope that they can both hold on long enough to get treatment.

"Thanks everyone for your help. Oh I almost forgot I am going to need a copy of that police and accident report." I tell them, and they radially agree. But now I just want to get to the hospital and I know Dakota is very anxious about them. The longer they are away from the hospital they less chance that they might

I get back to Dakota in my truck and I know she wants

me to tell her what I saw but I can't worry her like that. I just tell her it didn't look great. I see the ambulance that Royce is on pull out and head down the road. So I follow it. I know they are getting Lexi loaded up so I feel a little bit better about leaving the scene. I just need to get to the hospital quickly.

We pull in right behind Royce. I saw that Dr. Baxton was waiting for him. Well I think he was just waiting for one of them. I am semi happy that Royce got here first because it looks like Royce has a concussion, especially after he said that his head hurt, then he closed his eyes. Not the biggest problem. So that way they can treat him and then concentrate all bodies on Lexi when she rolls in. It wasn't more than five minutes before Lexi arrives at the ER.

I hate the hospital, its so sterile and its so noisy I don't know how anyone could get any rest. You have doctors and nurses always coming in to check vitals and they wake you up so you can tell them your name. Every two to three hours. How is a person supposed to get better and rest when the nurses and everyone is coming to check on them. If they are asleep let them sleep. Anyway back to Lexi. She doesn't look good at all. There is blood all over her. I have no clue where it is all coming from. I am so scared, not just for her, but for my brother and Dakota as well.

Lexi has been in the ER for a long time and no one has come out to tell us what is going on. Dakota is her emergency contact because they are always together so they should tell her whats happening and by default I will know as well because I am not letting her out of my sight. She needs me more now than before. Finally I see Dr. Baxton coming towards us. His look does not bode well for how this conversation is going to go. I stand from my chair and Dakota does the same. Dakota must realize that this is the doctor that was called in for Royce and Lexi. I have one arm around Dakota for comfort. I extend my other hand out to the doctor and he shakes it.

"Jaxson, I wish we were meeting under different

circumstances. And you must be Dakota, I have heard many good things about you. Again I am sorry we are meeting at a time like this."

"Hello, Dr. . Baxton." I say.

"Hello, Dr. Baxton." I hear Dakota say softly. She is trying to be strong but I don't know how much longer she can keep it together. We need to get this over with quickly.

"Dr. what can you tell us about Royce?" I ask.

"Royce seems to have a small concussion. He is very lucky since the car didn't land and drag on his side. He will be sore and bruised. Have a raging headache for probably about a week, may experience some dizziness but over all with rest and low stress he will fully recover." I sigh a huge relief. My brother is going to be okay.

Now Dr. Baxton turns slightly to Dakota. "Lexi suffered a head injury as well, her shoulder was disconsolate from hitting the side of the car when it flipped onto her side. The car dragged her in her seat belt but she did hit her head. The seat belt did its job to where she was kept in place, it locked like it was supposed to which is a good thing. The problem was that the placement of the seat belt was a little high on the abdomen. It looks like all of her reproductive systems bruised from the scan we did. I am sorry to tell you this but she lost the baby. Her body's instincts was to hemorrhage the blood and the baby in her uterus. I am sorry to deliver the bad news. By the looks on your faces you didn't know about the baby. She was ten weeks along and was very surprised when I told her earlier today. She will be getting settled into a room soon. I will come back and get you guys when both are settled." With that the doctor walked away. I yell out to Dr. Baxton. "Could you please put them in the same room. I know when one of them wakes up they will want to be with the other one." He nods and resumes his walk back to get everyone settled.

Dakota just loses it. I grab her and hold her tight. "Let it out baby. Let it out." I say to her as I rub my hands up and down her back. I don't know how long we were in each others arms. At this point we were both in our own worlds. We didn't say anything. All we did was hold each other and cry. I will admit I cried harder than I thought was possible. Our family was hurting and I don't know about Dakota but I was feeling useless and like I should be in there hurt with them or instead of them. I guess this is what survival guilt feels like. I know they are not dead but I still don't want them hurt.

"Honey, lets go get some air before we head up to see them. Dr. Baxton knows to call me if he doesn't see us."

"Sure. I could use some air." She says so quietly and hesitantly. I know she doesn't really want to go but I know it will be good for her.

As we head out of the hospital doors towards the car, her hand grips mine to the point of almost drawing blood. I look at her and she is pale. Well not just pale she as white as a ghost. I don't even need to ask her what is wrong. I feel him before I see him. Justin and Steve are out in the parking lot. This needs to stop.

"Well if it isn't the Devil himself." I say as we stop right in front of them.

"Watch it, I didn't think we would see you here." Justin says with a smug look on his face.

"Why wouldn't we be here, our family is in there no thanks to you." I am so angry, I am starting to not think straight.

"Royce wasn't supposed to be apart of this. It has only ever been about Lexi and how she can't have anyone since I threw her away."

"You want to know who else wasn't supposed to be apart of this?" Dakota sneers.

"Who?" Justin is flabbergasted.

"The baby you killed. Lexi was carrying your child you jackass. She was ten weeks along!"

"No, she couldn't have been carrying my child I always wore protection."

"Well I guess you had super sperm the last time you raped her."

He had no clue it is written all over his face. I get one last jab in before we get back to our family. "Get the hell out of our lives. Lexi doesn't want you and we don't want you!"

As soon as we get back in we tell the hospital security all of the information we can about Justin and Steve. They are not allowed anywhere near here. They readily agree. Just then my phone vibrates with a text message from Dr. Baxton. He must be using Royce's phone because it has Royces' name pops up. All it says is room 3214.

"Looks like we are going to level three to go see our family." I tell Dakota.

"Alright I need to see Lexi, and I know you need to see Royce. Lets go."

We get off the elevator and follow the signs on the walls about which way to these section of rooms and so forth. We finally find room 3214, the door is open so I take a quick glance to make sure its the correct room and my heart breaks for Royce and Lexi.

CHAPTER FORTY-FOUR

LEXI

Beep, Beep, Beep

Ugh what is that horrid sound, why can I not stop the banging in my head. I can't move my arms they are so heavy. What is going on? Why can I not remember what happened or where I am? Think Lexi what could have happened? Then last thing I remember is I was in the car with Royce. He was driving us to Taco Bell because I didn't want to go out with our family. I wanted to cry and not be with anyone, but why I can't remember. Oh this is so much work, I am going to go back to my happy black sleepy place.

CHAPTER FORTY-FIVE

ROYCE

O
h my head. Can someone please stop the pounding party that is going on in my head. I can't get my eyes open. But I hear beeping noise. I also hear whispers, people are talking. What are they talking about? Oh if they would just talk a little bit louder and a little bit closer to me. Time to go back to my dark sleepy place.

Beeping is all I hear, I try and wake up more, I have no clue what time it is or how long I have been out. I hear crying and hushed voices. I can just make out the voices. Its Dakota and Jaxson.

"Jaxson, whats wrong?" I can barely get it out. But I must have been loud enough because he comes rushing to my side.

"Oh I am so happy your awake. How do you feel? Do I need to get the nurse? Dakota can you grab the nurse just in case." He is rambling at a million miles an hour.

"I am fine, my head hurts but other than that I am okay. How long have I been out?" I ask.

"You have been out about a day. Man I was so scared for you and Lexi."

"Is Lexi going to be fine? I tried to stay conscious, but I couldn't. I feel horrible. I am sorry you guys had to wait for me and Lexi. I am the one who is supposed to make sure she is alright." I am kicking myself I needed to be stronger than I was.

"Royce you did the best you could in that situation. You made sure everyone who needed to be called was called. You even went above and called Dr. Baxton to make sure he was here. We were just scared for you two. Also. . ."

"Also what. What are you not telling me?"

"Well so far Lexi hasn't woken up yet, and when she does there is going to be some very bad news."

"What news. What happened to her?"

"She lost the baby. The seat belt wasn't low enough and when it tightened along with the jarring of the car it made her miscarried. Hence all of the blood that was in the car. None of her bones are broke, but she is going to be devastated."

"She lost the baby?"

"I am so sorry man, I didn't even know about the baby. I didn't know. I am so sorry, when did you find out?"

"We found out when we went to the doctor yesterday, it was yesterday right? I can't keep track a lot has happened in the last thirty-six hours."

"Yes it was yesterday. Just relax man." Jaxson said as he was patting my shoulder. The next thing I know the nurse is checking my vitals and then gives me some more medication and I fall back asleep. The last thought I had was I need to be awake when Lexi gets the news of the baby.

CHAPTER FORTY-SIX

LEXI

Groaning, I can't get into a comfortable position on this bed, the beeping noise is still so loud. I just want to be next to Royce and have him hold me. Someone is holding my hand. I turn slowly and see Dakota is the one who is holding my hand, and it looks like she has been crying.

"Dakota, whats wrong?"

"Dakota, its not our news to share. She needs to hear it from either the doctor or Royce. Plus, Royce needs to be awake for that conversation." Jaxson buts in.

"What is going on? My head is killing me can someone tell me why?"

"What do you remember Lexi?" Dakota is squeezing my hand when Jaxson asks me that question.

"I don't know, I know I was with Royce and we were on our way to Taco bell. We came from the doctor's office." Then it clicks I am supposed to be pregnant. "Can someone get the nurse for me I am thirsty."

"Sure I will go get her." Dakota says sadly.

"Jaxson has Royce been awake yet? I need him and I know he will need me." I am starting to panic.

"Lexi, Royce is across the room, you guys were lucky enough to be able to get a room together. Yes he has been awake. Please calm your breathing. Okay, breath with me. In and out there you go."

"Hello Lexi, I hear your thirsty, lets get you some ice chips. I don't want you to throw up. You have a sensitive tummy right now."

"What does she mean?" Jaxson isn't looking at me in the eye. This is a bad sign. I can't keep my mind on it because I hear movement in the other bed.

"Jaxson come help me." Royce says through gritted teeth.

"Should he be getting out of bed?" I ask the nurse. "No worries honey its good for him to get up and moving. That way I can take out his IV."

"Lexi, I am so happy to see you awake. How do you feel baby girl?"

"Royce, I feel better now that I can see you. Can you come lay in bed with me?"

"There is nothing more I would rather be doing."

"Jaxson I think now would be a good time to get the doctor don't you think?" Royce sends his brother to get Dr. Baxton.

"How are you feeling? Are you dizzy or hurting anywhere?"

"I am tired and my head hurts and it feels like I have cramps, but on a larger scale? That can't be good for the baby."

It was at that point in time when the doctor comes in. I swear he doesn't show emotion. I can't tell if this is going to be a good or a bad news visit. I am assuming that it is going to be a bad news visit because no one would tell me anything before the doctor came in.

"Hi Lexi, Royce. How are you two feeling?" We both confirm that we are sore and our heads hurt but I don't think its life and death. I guess that was the wrong phrase to say, because everyone went silent.

"Okay guys what is everyone not telling me."

Royce takes a huge sigh. "Lexi, the doctor has told us that you lost the baby. Everything that happened in the car was too much and the fetus was too young to survive the impact of the seat belt."

"I.... I am not pregnant anymore?"

"No, baby your not." As soon as Royce finish that statement, I just lost it. I am so sad that I am not pregnant anymore but I am happy that I won't be having Justin's baby. I don't know how I can be so conflicted. But I am so hysterical that Dr. Baxton has to give me something to calm myself down. I don't want everyone to feel sorry for me. I can feel the medicine working and my eyes get really heavy. Royce goes to get out of my bed and I just hold on tight. I need someone to hold onto.

CHAPTER FORTY-SEVEN

ROYCE

I feel so bad for my baby girl. She doesn't deserve everything that is happening to her. I know she is sad, but to what extent is what I am worried about. How am I supposed to be there for her, I know she is going to be pushing me away. I need to talk to Jaxson and Dakota about this, especially Dakota. Lexi has always felt like she had to take everything on her self and not ask for any help at all.

Finally I feel Lexi's body relax and I know she is in a deep sleep, even if it is medical induced. Now is the perfect time for me to slide out of her bed and have the conversation.

"Hey Jaxson, can you guys wait up for a second. I know you need to get back home and check on the ranch."

"Royce we are here for whatever you two need. If we need to be here then that is where we are going to be. Dakota will stay with Lexi and I can go check on all businesses. We are going to figure it out. What did you need to talk to us about?"

"I am really worried about Lexi. I need help in knowing what I need to be doing. Dakota do you have any insight? You are her best friend."

"Honestly Royce I am as lost as you are. Lexi and I never really talked about the hard emotional I need help issues. We both have baggage with family and always thought that we needed to take on the world by ourselves. I think the only advice I can give to all of us, is to let it play out. Be there for her but don't smother and if she says she is fine, and we know she isn't but we cannot pull it out of her. She will only retreat more into herself."

"Sounds good, we go at her pace. We need to patient. We love each other and we are going to be a family." Jaxson continues "We also need to be ready with distractions. Royce you might want to get ready for sleepless nights and/or nightmares."

"Okay as soon as she is ready I want to take her back to the bar. She deserves a night out of dancing and drinks with her loved ones."

"We are down with that. We are not going to make any plans so we can be what she needs. We have never lost a child so we don't know what she is going through but we can be supportive." Dakota speaks slowly and at a low level so no one can over hear our conversation.

"Okay so as long as we are all in agreement, you guys need to go get some food and check on everything. I need to get back in there and sneak back into the bed so she doesn't know I left for a bit."

As quietly and slowly that I can manage, I sneak back in and she cuddles back into me. She is my whole world, she never deserved anything that her life dealt her. I am so happy that it didn't take me long to figure it out. I am going to give her everything she deserves and then some. I can't wait to marry her.

CHAPTER FORTY-EIGHT

LEXI

As I start to wake up from whatever Dr. Baxton gave me, I hurt and for once it is not my body. It is my heart. I wanted a child and so when I found out I was pregnant I was over the moon until the other shoe dropped. I didn't want to carry Justin's baby, but I didn't want the baby to have to die either. My emotions are all over the place. I am so confused. Royce is still asleep next to me. I wonder how long I was asleep? I am scanning the room and no one is here, Jaxson and Dakota must have gone back home for the night. I am happy they need their rest.

A nurse quietly walks into our room and is happy to see that I am awake. "How are you feeling?" She asks me.

"I am fine I tell her, ready to go home. I will get much more rest when I am back on the ranch. When do I get to go home?" I ask.

"The doctor put in your chart that when you feel up to it then you can be released. Since it is two o'clock in the morning I think the earliest we can do is ten this morning.

We want to make sure you can keep down regular food since you haven't eaten for three days it looks like. Would you like anything?"

"Maybe some juice sounds good. Thank you."

"No problem I will be back as quick as I can."

I want to get out of bed but I don't want to wake up Royce, I start to slide out as carefully as I can, but it is not good enough. Royce grabs me and holds on tight. Now, I have no choice but to wake him up.

"Royce, wake up please."

"Hmm?"

"Wake-up, I need to go to the bathroom."

Just as I am trying to wake up Royce who is apparently really out of it. The nurse comes back in with my juice.

"Hey, can you help me get out of bed? I need to go to the bathroom."

"Sure." She says with a smile.

The only way to get me out from under Royce's arm is for her to lift it as I slide. Then she gently sets it back down on the bed and comes to help me stand. I have had lots of different drugs in me so I am a little wobbly on my feet. "Thank you. I won't be long and then I am just going to sit in this chair. Can I go for a walk in a little bit, I am kind of stiff and would like to stay out of the bed as much as possible."

"I don't see any problem with going for a walk. How about I come back in after I finish my rounds and then I will take you just in case you get dizzy again."

"I think that sounds like a fantastic plan."

Who knew doing nothing was so exhausting, I hurt but its manageable. A walk will do me good. Royce needs his sleep so I don't want to disturb him. He doesn't need to be in this position. If he wasn't with me then he would not have to deal with stupid people. I still have no clue as to why Justin just won't leave me alone. He never paid this much attention to me while we were dating. I mean nothing to him, he has made that clear on many occasions.

I am so lost in my thoughts that I didn't hear Royce moving in the bed. I barely hear what he is saying to me. "what are you doing up?"

"I had to go to the bathroom, go back to sleep its early still. I am going to go for a walk when the nurse comes back."

"I want to go with you."

"Its okay you need to rest. You have been through a lot. I will be fine with the nurse."

"Nonsense I am going to walk with you."

"Fine. I guess this way I don't have to wait for the nurse. She was only going to go with me encase I get dizzy again."

"You were dizzy, maybe you shouldn't go for a walk, you need to get back into bed."

"The only reason I was a little bit dizzy was because of all the different medicines they have been pushing through my IV."

As he is gritting his teeth he says, "fine we will take it slow there is no rush."

I pull out a small smile, but I am biting my tongue. I feel like he is going to ambush me and not leave me be. I need to get through this my own way. Yes I want him for support but I don't need to be suffocated. I can already feel him suffocating me. So how do I just tell him to back off. I mean I know when I woke up I grabbed for him for his love but now that I, myself do not understand what I am feeling or what is going on. A couple days ago I was pregnant and not happy about whose it was. But I loved the idea of me being pregnant with Royce's baby. I don't want to feel happy about not having Justin's baby inside me anymore, on top of the fact that he killed his own child. Does he even know? Would he even care, probably not.

"What is going on inside of your head baby?"

"I don't know what I am supposed to feel, everything I feel seems wrong. I know you want to help me but I also feel like you might try and suffocate me without meaning to. I want you to help me deal but I don't know how I am supposed to deal with all of this."

"Lexi, baby girl, I want to help you, I want to go at your pace. All I ask is that you don't push me away."

"I can't promise anything. I am trying to control my thoughts and I can't do it. I feel like I am a bad person for being happy that I no longer am caring Justin's baby, I am mad that he is the one who killed it and that he probably doesn't even care. But I am so upset and mad at the fact that I am no longer pregnant. None of this makes sense. I don't even think I am ready to be a mother, but I can't explain it."

"Baby girl, don't get yourself worked up please. You just found out. Your emotions are expected to be all over the place. Do you want us to speak to Dr. Baxton and see what our options are? If maybe you and I go talk to a counselor."

"Right now I just want to go back home, to our home. I want us to take a hot shower and then lay in bed. I want to forget. I can't deal with this right now."

"I understand. I want to go home as well with you and get you settled. Dakota and Jaxson are going to bring us food when we get home is there something special you want? Nothing is off limits."

"Potato soup sounds great. With sausage and cheese and huge chunks of potatoes and Texas toast or bread sticks." I say to Royce with a huge grin.

"That is very detailed and is sounds amazing. I am going to text Jaxson when we get back from our walk. I know its early but I am pretty sure we are going to be released today."

"Yeah, I already asked the nurse this morning when she helped me to the bathroom."

"How long was I out while you were awake. I don't know how I feel about you being alone while I am sleeping. Next time can you wake me up as well?"

"No, you need your sleep and rest as well since you got the worse from the wreck."

"We are not going to argue about this. If you are awake so am I. Or even better we will have Dakota and Jaxson stay with us for the first few days. You are not to be the only one up. I know the ranch has security but we are not taking any chances."

"That is crazy. We will be fine. We do not need to upend their lives as well. People are on the ranch all the time working. I won't be the only one awake. Honey, you are starting to be more than suffocating me. Please can we just take this one day at a time?"

"Okay lets start when we get home. Oh look I think our doctor is awaiting our return."

As we approach our room, Dr. Baxton is in deed waiting for us. He says he discharged us and that we need to take it easy. Also, he is going to come check on us at the ranch in a couple of days since neither one of us is cleared to drive. The main and most important thing he harpped on the most is that both of you need to be stress free and heal for a few more days before bringing any other doctors or medical professionals."We say our thanks and see ya later. I get a hold of my brother and Dakota and tell them the request on food, and also that we are going to be getting the boot from here so if they could please come and pick us up that would be great. I can't wait for my own bed.

As the day progresses I can tell that Lexi is in her head. I can feel her body shaking against me but I don't want to point it out because I don't want her to get more stressed out. I am trying not to suffocate her but I can feel her shutting down. But I am going to do what I said we are going to go home shower get settled and then food will be brought to us.

"Ready to wash the hospital off of us?"

"Oh yes, I can't stand myself. How can you stand to be so close to me I must smell really bad."

"No matter how bad you think you smell I will always be holding you close to me."

"You say the most kind words to me."

"It's only because I love you so much." It is time to change the direction of the conversation and my opening just walked through the door. "Oh, look our getaway car is here. Lets hurry and hit the road. Well at least as fast as we can."

"Okay speed demon lets go, I want to get some real food in me, and a real bed."

Just as we leave our room we see Dakota and Jaxson head our way. "A little anxious to leave I see?" Jaxson says with his eye brow raised.

Lexi jumps in saying that she was ready to go at three this morning. "Well I am glad they waited until at least nine." Dakota laughs.

"I haven't showered in days, I want to get the smell off of me and in my own bed." Lexi sighs. "I am sorry I didn't mean to snap. I just want to go. Please?" I don't know what is ahead of me but I am not going to leave Lexi's sight. I hope that doesn't push her away from me.

CHAPTER FORTY-NINE

ROYCE

As we are leaving the room and headed for the exit of the hospital Dakota moves into mother hen mode with, "Jaxson I am going to sit in the back of the truck with Lexi, we could use some girl talk. You boys behave up in the front seat." I feel like she is speaking in a way to convey a message and I am have no clue what she is talking about, so I hope Jaxson knows what she is talking about. Thankfully Jaxson gets it. "That sounds like a great idea honey. Royce and I need to talk about some stuff that has to concern the ranch anyway."

The girls are in the truck and I just look at him. "What Ranch business do we need to discuss?" I level him with a glare. He comes back with "look this way Lexi is more apt to open up about how she is feeling and then Dakota will come to us and maybe not walk on egg shells all the time."

"Okay that is a great plan. I can't believe I didn't come up with that."

"Its fine you have kind of had blinders on with that.

You are in the moment kind of guy who can think quickly on his feet, but this isn't going to be a quick fix. Plus, Lexi needs her best girl friend. You are not that. You are her best friend but not a girl."

CHAPTER FIFTY

LEXI

I have a feeling that Dakota is going to want to talk and that is the last thing I want to do. I just want to understand what I am supposed to feel. I want to be mad, I want them to let me be mad. I want to not talk about it, and not talk at all really until I can wrap my head around this.

"Hey Lexi, how are you feeling?" Dakota asks me. Ugh I hate that question, I can't give a straight answer to her.

"Fine." That is the best I can do. No, I am not fine I am far from it. But no one is going to really understand what feelings I have going on in my head. Dakota has never been pregnant, nor a stalker ex. I am still trying to figure out how he got our of jail that quickly, but I should just know that money talks. Anyway brain get back on track.

Dakota is so sad when she starts talking to me again. "Hey, I can see your not fine, I want to help. The guys want to help. Royce is beside himself with this whole thing."

Looking out the window I let out this long sigh. "Look

Dakota I can't tell you how I am, I can't wrap my head around these different feelings I am having. Physically as long as I have my pain meds I will be fine. Mentally I just don't want to talk about anything. I am sorry if that sounds bitchy but I am sorry. Please respect my wishes." With that little speech I closed my eyes for the rest of the way back to the ranch. Please don't let the nightmares come to me while I am in the car. I don't want everyone to see.

CHAPTER FIFTY-ONE

DAKOTA

I wait until I know she is asleep, and then lean up to the front of the seats. "Hey guys, this is not going to be easy. I don't know what we should do. I feel like if we respect her wishes, she is going to push everyone away. But if we don't respect her wishes then she will push everyone away that much faster. Does that make sense?"

Jaxson is the first to respond to my open ended question. "Yes, and no. Plus it also depends on what she wants."

"Yeah what does she want?" Royce chimes in.

I sigh, "she wants us to not talk about it or even make her talk. She wants to process and retreat into her head. She said physically she will be fine that is a no brainier but mentally she doesn't know where to start in processing everything. I think she is sad and happy at the same time, and also really mad. Knowing her the way I do, I can almost think she is happy that she is not pregnant by him any more but she is mad that she isn't pregnant. Does this make sense?"

This time Royce beat Jaxson to the punch. "Yes, I remember we found out she was pregnant we were both happy, but when we asked how far along, she just shut down. She didn't want to talk about it."

We were still a little bit away from the ranch and I hear mumbling words and moans coming from Lexi. I can tell she is still asleep and something is haunting her. "Hey," I gently shake her awake. "Hey we are almost at the ranch come one sleepy head wake up. You can go back to sleep as soon as you take a bath and eat some food."

"Hmm, oh we are here aren't we. I see the gates, thanks for waking me Dakota." She smiles at me. I am not going to tell her about the dream, I know she remembers it but doesn't want to talk about it.

CHAPTER FIFTY-TWO

LEXI

Pulling in front of the house I just want to get into the huge shower and wash away hospital smell.

"Thank you Jaxson and Dakota for coming to our rescue. I think I am going to go hit the shower."

Jaxson answers for both himself and Dakota. "It was our pleasure, if you need anything call us and we will bring it. I hear dinner is going to be potato soup with sausage and cheese, with a bread roll or stick of some kind. I can not wait."

"Yep I got the recipe off someones board on Pintrest. I started it in the slow cooker so it should be done by five or five-thirty." Dakota announces.

Royce goes over and hugs her and Jaxson. "Thanks again guys. It is going to be weird not being able to drive."

"That is the point. No driving means forcing you to relax and heal. The no driving also means do not operate any heave machinery. Now go with your girl and help her in the shower and to bed. We will bring some munchie foods for you guys to snack on until dinner comes tonight."

Jaxson says with an authoritative voice.

We watch what Jaxson has deemed our family walk out the door. "It's so good to be home." I say to Royce.

"I know right. Come on we need to get showered and back to resting. We can put a movie on if you want?"

"No, I think I just want to lay down." This way he can't make me talk about things I don't want to.

"Okay, let's go."

CHAPTER FIFTY-THREE

ROYCE

I know she is only wanting to lay down so she won't have to talk about stuff. I can be okay with that for today but tomorrow is going to be a different story.

"Hey baby, I have an idea. I read a book about someone who went through some trauma and it helped if they wrote in a spiral book things that was hard to talk about. I have an extra spiral notebook in my office, what if we put it on your side of the bed and you can write down what ever is in your thoughts. You can share it with me or not, but this way you can rotate your thoughts and not going over and over about the same phrase or thought."

"I really like that idea. I don't know how much I will want to actually talk about this since I don't know what or how I am supposed to feel. This could give me an outlet with out pressure."

"Okay we can get it after our nap. That hot water is calling our name." Lexi says halfheartedly.

"Sounds like a plan. Please don't shut me out. I want to

help you anyway I can."

"One day at a time, that is all I can do. But, don't take this the wrong way but, I am done talking for a while."

I reach for her and pull her into me for a long embrace. I don't want to let go, as long as I have a hold on her then she can't push me away. "In you go baby girl. The water is just right. Hot to help to heal our muscles. How does your shoulder feel? We have been so focused on the fact that your not pregnant anymore, that I totally forgot your shoulder was dislocated." I climb in after her but have Lexi sit forward so her back can rest against my front. It just happens to be my favorite way to hold her.

"My shoulder is fine. It is sore but manageable. I just need to take some ibuprofen 800. Dr. Baxton said it would help with inflammation to go down. I also should put some ice on it but that can wait until after our nap."

"Okay." I utter. "Rest your eyes, there is nothing for you to worry about. You are safe here with me."

Lexi feel asleep in my arms while we are in the bath. He brain needs to catch up so she can tell me how she is really doing. I know she is happy and sad at the same time. I myself am angry. I am so angry that I want to murder someone, and by someone I mean Justin. He gives the whole male species a bad rap.

CHAPTER FIFTY-FOUR

LEXI

When Royce told me I couldn't leave the ranch without either him or Jaxson, at first I was not happy at all. I mean I knew I could keep myself occupied with the event coming up but still, I didn't want to be grounded. At the time I got the impression there was something everyone wasn't telling me. I let it go and told myself to just go with the flow. Well now that I am really ranch bound and almost bed bound due to stupid Justin. I hate the fact that he got to us. He hurt Royce. Royce told me that he loved me. And then we get into the accident. Maybe now he won't love me anymore. I don't want that to happen but I would understand. Its been a couple of days since we have been back and I am enjoying my long walks around the ranch.

The ranch was stunning. Thankfully, the weather was nice and it hadn't been too hot. There were shades browns and greens on the ground, and the trees are all different colors of reds and oranges. I wish I knew the different type of trees. The barn was the normal red color and I could hear the horses in there. I tried to stay out of the way of the guys who worked at the JBR, they were nice to me and I was even allowed to pet some of the animals and give them treats. Some of the animals were out roaming the area. Cows grazing lazily out in the pastures, with not a care in the world if they were fed and watered. Everything was fine in their world.

In the week to come, I need to finish all the plans for the event. Oh, man I need to get off this ranch. It is starting to look like a cow has a better life than I do, and he is going to end being someone's dinner.

Since I haven't left the ranch at all, means I haven't heard anything from Justin. Royce and I ate all meals in the kitchen, and we only watch movies in his personal theater. The walls of the house have begun to start closing in on me. A person can only take so much of the same thing. I can feel myself fill with energy and become stir crazy. I have finished all the planning for the event and luckily we will be leaving in a few days. Don't get me wrong I love being on this ranch and it seems to fit me perfectly. Royce and I sleep together every night, but nothing happened besides a few passionate kisses before bed. He would spend the rest of the night holding me. I haven't slept this well since my childhood.

During my normal walk around the ranch, my cell phone beeps. I am used to Royce checking on me. I grab my phone and my face falls. Instead of a kind text from Royce, this is what I see.

Justin: Bitch, do you know where your boyfriend is? Shouldn't he be home by now?

Royce was cleared to drive two days ago and so he had to run some errands. So, just as I am about to call Royce his name pops up on my screen, and I smile.

"Hey Royce, where are you at?"

"I just pulled down the drive. Why do you ask?"

"I just got a weird text from Justin, he made it seem like

you were hurt or with someone else."

Royce lets out a heavy sigh informs me that he had some news that he needs to share with me.

This can't be good. I thought we had all agreed to just wait it out, but it seems like Justin is not going to be giving up anytime soon.

"I will meet you in the kitchen. I have a roast slow cooking in the Crock-Pot, and it should be done now." I tell him.

I have been taking over all the cooking because let's face it I have nothing better to do all day, since I still can't leave without a chaperon. I shouldn't be resentful, but I am starting to be. I resent Royce for keeping me locked up on this ranch of his, but most of all I resent Justin for doing this to me in the first place. I always think it is best to talk things over with a nice home-cooked meal. Hopefully this won't be bad news. What am I thinking... if Justin is involved it will be bad news.

CHAPTER FIFTY-FIVE

ROYCE

I know as soon as I tell Lexi about the meetings I have been having with Dakota and Jaxson she is going to bolt out the door and not look back. Jaxson and I decided to dig deeper into Justin's history, and the results came back; there are some things I believe Lexi needs to know. Of course, I am going to sugar coat it.

When I walk into the kitchen Lexi is dishing up or dinner. This isn't dinner conversation, but it is a conversation we needed to have. "Justin is a psychopath who will not stop until he gets what he wants," I blurt out.

"Wh...What did you say? Do you know what he wants with me?" Lexi questions.

"That is the problem Jaxson, Dakota, and I are working on," I reply.

"What! Why are you guys not letting me in on your secret meetings? I mean, it is my life that is in danger. With the three of you plotting to keep me safe, when I have no clue? What happened to 'we will all figure this out together.' I am not a child. I can take care of myself! I have been doing it my whole life since my parents were always too busy being in the social spotlight," Lexi screams!

When she is finished, she backs her chair out with so much force it falls over backwards.

"I should have known all along this was going on, but no, you wanted to keep me in the dark. Well, no more! I am out of here whether you like it or not. I can keep myself safe; I have been doing it for years since my parents were always too busy with their own careers and social functions," Lexi angrily paces back and forth. And with that she walks out of the house. She doesn't want to hear it, so she walked out. I understand her being upset and the need to feel included, I am worried about her safety. I felt it would scare her more than she was already. I will give her credit. She hid it well. I reach for my cell and call the guard house and tell them to keep an eye on her but do not stop her. She needs her space.

"Sir, we tried to contact you with text and a phone call but there was no answer." one of the guards tell me.

"Why would you need to contact me?" This is when they inform me Justin has been driving around the ranch waiting for someone to leave. He is following behind Lexi in his car.

Hearing this makes my blood boil. I slam the phone down and run to my truck. I need to make sure nothing happen to Lexi. Justin is a big fan of chicken if I remember correctly. Right after the lawsuit and before my parents died, there had been more than one occasion where I was driving along and he would come at me going the wrong way in my lane. But at the last second he would swerve off. One of these days he is going to lose.

Thankfully, Lexi makes it all the way to the diner. I debate going in and talking to her, but it's probably best I don't. She's too worked up to hear anything I have to say. Even though I know she's being a bit irrational, she's Lexi – and I'm coming understand and appreciate that. To her, everything matters, and that's okay. I just wish she knew how much I've grown to care about her. Beyond my issues with Justin and Lexi's general safety, I care.

I know the last thing she wants is my help, and maybe I went about this wrong, but I didn't want to fight her on this. Besides, not even Dakota knows everything. I am going to have to talk to Jaxson about informing the girls about our money and position while on this trip, but it's never a good time to say "Oh by the way I am rich, like Bill Gates rich." Granted, I know we can trust Lexi and Dakota. Maybe we will just get through Chicago and then play it by ear.

CHAPTER FIFTY-SIX

LEXI

Pure rage fuels my journey as I start walking ten miles to the diner. When I found about Royce meeting with Dakota and Jaxson behind my back, I felt betrayed. I know they all mean well, but this is ridiculous. Don't they understand that this is my life, and even if the Justin situation is getting out of hand, I can handle it. I know I cry and I lose control of my emotions a lot, but I am capable of handling my life. I feel embarrassed and hurt. I have to get out of Royce's house. I need to be away from all of this. I walk down the long dirt drive to the main road. I don't look back. I am sure the guards have called Royce, but I don't care. I can hear a car following me, I know it is going to be one of two people. Justin or Royce. I am too scared to turn around to see which one it is. The car continues to follow me, and when I went to cross the road I saw red out of the corner of my eye. I am tired of running and I just want to be done. I don't want to be scared but I am human and I am terrified. I just have to keep pretending that I am strong.

The funny thing is he is keeping his distance as he drives behind me. This is totally unlike the Justin I dated. I am tired of being trapped. I am not going to be anyone's puppet ever again.

During my walk, I start to calm down. By the time I reach the diner my rage has turn to embarrassment for the way I acted. Ugh they should not have kept me out of the loop. I am not that fragile. I know they are only trying to protect me, but I am not used to that. Regardless of their intentions, I should have been included in their plans since I am the one with the crazy ex-boyfriend; he is trying to hurt me not them. Literally.

I walk into the diner and take the booth all the way in the back. I notice Royce's vehicle pull up and park. He parks right next to Justin's car. I wish Justin would get over me and move on to his next victim. I want my life back. I want to finally be in a healthy and sexual relationship with Royce, tell him how much he meant to me and thank him for protecting me. I am supposed to be in Chicago in a few days. A lot of people are counting on Dakota and I. We are planning the annual fundraiser for the Chicago aquarium's program Dream to Believe. This great program allows everyone a chance to experience the aquarium.

As I sit in the booth staring out the window at their vehicles I notice a shadow out of the corner of my eye. I glance up to see Dakota standing next to my table when did she get here?As I turn and continue staring out the window Justin's car backs out of the parking lot.

"Are you going to ignore the fact I am standing right here?" Dakota whines.

"No, but I thought you came to see me so you could start the conversation, because I am still furious you. You guys took it upon yourselves to treat me like a child and not talk to me about all this craziness happening. Not you but me!" At this point I am yelling at my best friend and that's not like me I need to get my emotions under control.

"We thought we were helping you. Maybe we should have consulted with you, but with the car still in the shop and Justin being crazy, we didn't want to cause you any more stress than you already had," Dakota explains sympathetically.

"Thanks for that." I say sarcastically. "Now knowing you guys were plotting stuff behind my back is putting more stress on me. Can you just let me have my peace and quiet."

"If you need me, you know where to find me." Dakota whispers.

After D leaves a waitress comes and takes my order. "I will have a coke and a piece of apple pie with a scoop of ice cream on top."

I am wishing I would not have ran off from Royce's house without my laptop or at least some paper and a pen. Maybe I can ask the waitress for some paper and a pen, this way I can start to write down the thoughts running through head.

"Hello Lexi."

"Oh good gravy are you guys lined up outside to make sure I am okay?"I am in no mood. I want to scream at him to leave me alone, but before I get the words out Royce sits down across from me. The waitress quickly returns to my table and takes his order.

"Um, I didn't know I asked you to stay and have pie with me." I sneer.

"I knew you wouldn't, but the truth is you can't get rid of me that easily. If it is the last thing I do, I am going to protect you. I know you're supposed to be in Chicago this next week, but do you think it is wise to go?I don't."

"Of course you don't," I raise my voice, drawing alarmed looks from the staff. Lowering my voice, I continue. "Now you are interfering with my business? I am going to go to Chicago, and I am going to fulfill the contract and make this fundraiser the best party they hired me for. I have everything lined up so it shouldn't be too hard. I know what I want everything to look like. I have already been paid so canceling is not an option. So, what are you going to do now, huh? Royce?"

CHAPTER FIFTY-SEVEN

ROYCE

I am going to take you back to the ranch, Jaxson and I will accompany you girls to Chicago, and we will be your personal body guards," I snap.

Lexi and I are staring each other down We are so caught up in our verbal battle that we missed our pie being delivered to our table. "Do I have any say in this?"

"Well...Lexi, since I can't talk you out of going, no you don't," I reply.

"How many times do I have to tell you? I do not need this kind of protection. I can take care of myself! You guys can't just up and leave, can you? What about your businesses? wouldn't that mean my car would not be done when I returned and I would still be stuck in this town?"

"Lexi, honey, I need you to come back to the ranch with me. I understand why you are mad about this. We should have never kept any of this from you. I was trying to make everything go away. Since that didn't work I did the next best thing, so I thoughtat the time, and kept you in the dark. I'm sorry, and I hope you can forgive me."

"Promise me, Royce, you won't keep things from me?"

I reach for Lexi and pull her out of the booth into a hug. "Come on let's go home." As I am helping Lexi into my truck, I hear a large truck coming down the road but I think nothing of it. No one notices Justin because he is not in his Porsche. Somehow he was able to get a large pickup truck. All of the sudden this truck pulls up behind us ramming the back-quarter panel of my truck sending it spinning. I have to jump out of the way so I am not hit by my own out of control car. I get a good look at the driver of the truck. I can not believe my eyes. Justin. How in the hell did he get a truck that fast. It was only about a half hour from the timehe left until we were getting into my car to go to the ranch. I am furious all I see now is red. I didn't even get the door shut before my car is hit. All I can hear is Lexi screaming, "Royce, why are we spinning?"

I wanted to answer her, but I can't get to her. I can still hear her screaming, "Royce! I can't get out of the car..."

I watched in horror as my range rover spun with the woman I loved in it, I feel so helpless. All the while Justin just hops out of his newly acquired vehicle to watch the mayhem. One of the ladies from the diner has come out and she tells me that the cops and ambulance are on its way. Justin must have over heard this. He jumps back into the truck and takes off. I don't care because all I can think about is my Lexi, my baby girl. She has to be okay, she just has to.

It seems to take forever before it comes to a stop, but in all actuality it only took a few minutes. As soon as it does, I ran up to Lexi's door. "Lexi! Lexi! Lexi, wake up baby girl. Please wake up baby girl." I yelled out frantically.

By this time I have died a million deaths, but I do hear the sirens and they are coming closer. Thank goodness.

Time stands still until she opens her eyes. "What the heck just happened?" Lexi spats out.

The police and the ambulance just got here. So before I

get pushed out of the way, I ask her:

"How are you feeling?" I questioned Lexi.

"My head hurts but other than that I think I am okay."

Sir, I hear the EMT say to me. He is wanting me to move so they can get Lexi out of the car and evaluate her and her injuries.

"I am going to be right back, I need to go call Jaxson to come tow and pick us up." I tell Lexi,

My hand is about to be forced. I whip my phone out of my pocket to call Jaxson. I need a tow truck to pick up my truck and I needed him to pick us up from the diner.

"Hey, Jaxson. Lexi and I had a bit of a problem down here at the diner. Can you and Dakota come pick us up and send a tow for my Rover?" I ask.

"Uh, yeah. We will be there as quickly as we can. Your gonna have to fill us in on the story at a later time." Jaxson confusedly.

"Probably won't have time until we are on our way to Chicago." I reply.

"Okay, be there as shortly." Then Jaxson hung up the phone.

I walk back over to where Lexi is sitting on the edge of the ambulance, and answering all the different questions. I can tell that the EMTs want her to go to the hospital, and she is refusing adamantly. I watch as the EMTs finally agree and she signs a piece of paper saying she is refusing treatment. I tell the EMTs that I will make sure to call Doctor Baxton to have her checked out. That seemed to placate them a little bit more.

As she starts to stand, she is a little wobbly, but I am right there to steady her. She smiles sheepishly at me and the EMTs. Wow this women is more stubborn, that even I am. How is it that I keep forgetting that fact.

While we are waiting for my brother and her best friend, the tow cops walk over to us after studying the scene. We give our statements of how there was another vehicle that took off when the mention of law enforcement being called in. We tell them the make of the truck and hit us, and the name of the driver. We also inform them at this time that he has been making threats and harassing Lexi. This is when I notice the officer who is a good family friend of ours looks at me. I try to make a motion that wont catch Lexi off guard but I fail.

"Royce, what is that look about?"

The officer now realizes that he made a mistake. She doesn't know. Well I guess now is as good time to tell her as any. It just so happens that Jaxson and Dakota shows up, so we only have to get this part over with one time.

"Hey Dakota, you guys made good time. I was just about to tell Lexi something really important."

"Royce, why did the officer make a gesture when Justin's name was mentioned." Lexi asks again, in almost a demanding tone.

Jaxson just caught on to what is about to happen.

Taking a very deep breath, I start. "We know Justin and his family. We had done some dog breeding for his parents. They were unhappy with the results and took us to court. We lost that portion of our business, but the worst part of it, was that my parents death wasn't too long after all of this went down. It was never proved but Jaxson and I think the Kramer family was in on the 'accident' our parents were in." I huff out in one breath. Thankfully Jaxson takes over for me. "This is why we want to keep both of you girls safe. We are very protective of people we love and care about."

Both girls are quiet, like they are taking it all in word for word. I guess the officer decided this was a good place to jump back in and ask more specific questions. Lexi starts from the beginning and then I fill in on what I know of their situation. He is jotting down notes so fast. We also tell him the last place we knew he was staying. So hopefully they will go and check that out.

After the officers decide that we can head home so Lexi can try and get some rest. The four of us pile into Jaxson's truck and head back to the ranch.

The girls are silent so I turn to Lexi, and ask her. "What were you saying about not needing protection?She doesn't answer me. She stars straight out the window. Finally she asks the million dollar question. No pun intended.

"Royce why did you and Jaxson not tell us?"

"Jaxson and I didn't know if Justin was here for us or you in the beginning. I had gotten a strange call that day before I went to the dinner to meet you for lunch. But, then I saw you through the window how you were kneeling on the ground and he whispered something in your ear. But, I still didn't know if or how the two were connected. That was the why we didn't tell you before now. We are sorry." More silence in the cab of the truck. I can't take it anymore, so I break the silence. "Lexi, do you trust me?"

"Trust you? Of course, I trust you or else I would have left a long time ago. I can't imagine not trusting you. You keep saving my life," Lexi answers, laughing nervously.

"We will be leaving in an hour, so pack your bags. Don't worry about Dakota and Jaxson. They already know the plan and they are on board with it."

"Oh great, another secret meeting. I wish I wasn't the last to know everything," Lexi whines.

"No it's not a surprise. Since both of our cars are at the shop, I decided to charter a flight to Chicago so you can do your fundraiser."

"Um, excuse me, no! I cannot afford a charter flight to Chicago. Dakota and I just started this business. By charting a flight, we are going to be hemorrhaging money. With that our business goes under. I can't believe Dakota said she was okay with this, even if we split the cost of chartering the flight it will still cost us too much money. We will rent a car. That will be less expensive, end of discussion."

"Sorry to tell you this, but we are not renting a car. That would be too dangerous. The plane is paid for and it's waiting for us at the airport. Do not worry about the cost. It's a friend of a friend's plane and we are getting the family special. Just be ready to go in forty-five minutes," I say smugly.

CHAPTER FIFTY-EIGHT

LEXI

Once we return to the ranch after Justin tried to kill me again, I walked into the house screaming, "I am so done with all of this!" After announcing my displeasure, I scurry up the stairs.

Dakota marches up the stairs after me and finds me throwing my clothes into a suitcase.

"Lexi! Lexi, what are you doing?"

"I don't know where Royce gets off being able to act like my father! I am out of here. I should have never forgiven Royce at the diner! I knew he couldn't stop hiding things."

"Look Lexi, I am your best friend. The guys just dropped a huge bombshell on us. This is for the best. We need to listen to them. They want to keep us safe."

"What so you are in on everything," I bellow. "Do you not understand that something isn't quite right with Justin? This is more than a twisted ex taunting you. After what the guys told me, I really believe he tampered with your car. It makes sense. And Lexi, if we hadn't been able to pull over safely or if Royce wasn't there when that creep tried to attack you in the restroom ... I just don't know. I don't know what could've happened to you, and you may not want to think about it, but he might be out to harm you. Like – really – harm you. You could be dead if it wasn't for Royce."

What!!! Why would Justin want to kill me?

"He is only trying to scare me. Justin wouldn't kill me, hurt me a little maybe, but not kill me," I whisper.

Dakota walks up to me and puts her arms around me.

CHAPTER FIFTY-NINE

ROYCE

After about thirty minutes I walk up the stairs and find Lexi and Dakota embracing in a hug. I don't want to interrupt. I stand in the doorway wishing it was me who had my arms around Lexi. We haven't been able to talk about our relationship at all. I hope that she remembers that everything that I am doing is because I love her. I know that Jaxson and Dakota are on my side and knows not to say anything about the details of this trip. We have two rooms and Jaxson will stay with Dakota. Well they have been pretty much joined together. Lexi and I will have the other suite. She probably thinks she will be rooming with Dakota, but again she is going to be mistaken. This is the only way I know that she will be safe. I need to be with her and hold her in my arms.

I stand in the doorway until I feel like I am stalking the girls and then I clear my throat. Both girls jump.

"I don't want to interrupt, but we do need to get going.

I want to try and sneak out of here before Justin knows we left."

"Keep your shorts on, this was short notice. I had to make sure I had everything." Lexi states.

"I'm sorry. Next time there is a maniac after you I will let you take your time so you can be sure to have everything," I state sarcastically

After making sure we all have everything we need, we make our way to the airport. The flight is going to take almost five hours.

The flight was uneventful. Thank goodness, I am not sure how much more I can handle. I know I have been strong for Lexi, but I am starting to get jumpy myself. Justin is starting to get to me. I have this nagging feeling something is going to happen. While the girls are occupied with the fundraiser I am going to talk to Jaxson about it. I don't know how much more any of us can take.

CHAPTER SIXTY

LEXI

The plane was amazing. It had six tan leather seats, and in the back, there was a king size bed for longer flights. Man, too bad I didn't want to join the mile-high club this would be the ideal plane to do it in! There was a spacious bathroom, not like the cramped squares on normal planes, and the galley kitchen was stocked with every snack and beverage imaginable. There was enough soda and booze to float an army.

The flight from Helena took about five hours, it was midnight by the time we made it to our motel in Chicago. I was exhausted and slept most of the trip.

When we land, I awake to Royce whispering in my ear, "Wake up sleepy head."

"Are we here already?" I ask sheepishly.

"Yep, we need to gather our luggage and get to our hotel."

"Um...hotel? We are staying at Motel 5 in downtown."

"There has been a change of plans. That motel was too far away from the aquarium for you to come and go safely.

We are staying at the Hyatt. It is still about a mile away, but I think it should be okay. Just remember you girls are not allowed to be out by yourselves. We are not taking any chances. We might have gotten out under the radar but I am not underestimating Justin anymore."

Really? Royce is going down this road again?Looking at Dakota, I nod my head. "We understand."

It was just after midnight by the time we are all checked in. All I want to do is curl up with Royce and have him hold me.

CHAPTER SIXTY-ONE

ROYCE

I know Lexi isn't going to take the change of accommodations well, but after about thirty minutes of arguing with her I finally get her to see why it is important to stay closer to the party venue. I am hopeful Justin will not follow us here to Chicago, but I have to be prepared if he does. Jaxson and I hire extra security for the night of the party. The party is being held at the aquarium, in the Kovler Hall's main foyer so it will be an open area. Even though the aquarium will be closed and this party is invitation only, I still can't take any chances. I want this party to be a success for Lexi and Dakota. I will do whatever I can behind the scenes to make sure that happens.

CHAPTER SIXTY-TWO

LEXI

Since it is so dark and I am exhausted as we pull up to the hotel I don't pay too much attention to the outside of the hotel. When we walk in to the lobby, I freeze. Oh my gosh...I have died and gone to heaven. This hotel is amazing! If I am dreaming I hope no one wakes me up. Royce and Jaxson make reservations at the Hyatt since it is down the street from the aquarium where we are holding the fundraiser. Through my sleepy eyes the lobby looks very modern, it has wood paneling around the whole area and whie floors, along with a sleek reservation desk. The wall behind the desk is brightly lit up. It makes the whole area appear huge. When we walk into the hotel I look to my left and there is a concierge desk, I have only seen one of these in the movies. Dakota and I sit on chairs in a seating area while Royce and Jaxson go and check in. I turned my head to the left and gaze at the back of Royce while he is talking to the person working the front desk. He catches me checking him out when he turns around and starts walking towards Dakota and I.

"Are you girls ready to go to our rooms?" Royce asks us.

We both just shake our heads. I am too tired and stressed to inquire about any of this. We travel down a hallway to the elevators and we entered when the doors open. I noticed Jaxson pushes the button that read suites. Royce passes Jaxson a key card and a smile spread across his face. I am too tired right now to ask any question, but I will get to the bottom of all this.

When the elevator reaches the top and, the doors open. I exit first and turn left and continue walking, I don't even know what room I am walking towards. Everyone else walked out behind me. Jaxson and Dakota stroll hand in hand the opposite way I am heading. Royce walks up behind me and grabbed my hand and spins me around, "Lexi, we are this way."

"I didn't know where I was going, but I needed to walk."

Royce puts his arm behind my back and guides me in the direction of our room. I follow his guiding and we walk to our room without a word. When we arrived at the door Royce put the key card in the door and unlocks it.

CHAPTER SIXTY-THREE

ROYCE

Lexi has been quiet since landing at the airport. She hasn't said anything at all since we had arrived at the hotel. Granted I'm sure she is overwhelmed with this place. I know she is going to freak out...

"Oh my gosh, Royce. This is room is gorgeous!" Lexi squeals.

Yes, it is. Well, she sounds happy. At least she didn't freak out like I thought she would.

The Hyatt has just completed a remodel and they have added an additional tower of rooms and the suites we were staying in. The whole hotel has a modern appearance. When we walk into our room I notice a short wall with the flat screen T. V. dividing the sleeping area from the sitting area.

"Hey Lexi, I am going to take a quick shower before I lay down," I announce.

She sitting on the edge of the bed when she responds, "Uh-huh."

CHAPTER SIXTY-FOUR

LEXI

After Royce announces he is taking a shower, a light bulb clicks in my head... A quick shower, huh? Yeah, I don't think so...

I quickly undress and waiting until I hear the water going. I then count to ten slowly. I don't want to chicken out, but tonight Royce and I are going to take our relationship to the next level. I hope anyway. I reach for the door handle to the bathroom. Yes, he left it unlocked. I nervously stroll to the shower curtain and peak through the small opening. Royce has his back to me. Perfect! I have no idea how to seduce a man, but hopefully I will not make a fool out of myself. I open the curtain just enough for me to step into the tub with him. He has his head down letting the water fall onto his back of his head and down his back. I reach my hands up to grab his arms. He must have sensed me because he doesn't jump at all, he rounds his neck to the left and gives me the smile that melts my heart. "Since I was going to take a quick shower as well, I thought I would combine mine with yours," I state shyly.

"Baby girl, I don't think it is going to be a quick shower." Royce answered with a seductive smile.

Oh, yes!

Royce turns and embraces me. I lie my head on his shoulder. I totally do not want this feeling to end. I love when he embraces me, I feel so safe, so secure. Royce softly kisses my lips. Deepening the kiss, a moan escapes from my lips, "Mmm." I can feel the vibration between our lips. Royce turned us around so I am facing the cascading water. Stepping back, I allow the water to run down my head and back. He reaches behind himself and grabs the shampoo. He begins to gently massage my scalp with it, all the while still kissing me. This is totally something out of a romance novel. I quickly grab some shower gel and washed myself off. I close my eyes, and I can feel Royce watching me. As I am finishing, he reaches around me and turns the water off. I grab a towel and quickly cover my front. Suddenly I feel self-conscious. Royce hands me the white fluffy robe he brought in for himself and smiles at me. I quickly snatch it out of his hands and put it on and I wrapped my hair with the towel. Royce puts a towel around his hips and walks out of the bathroom and shuts the door. I quickly brushed my hair out and dry it. I hate going to bed with my hair wet. I also apply some of my favorite body lotion, ironically named Mad About You. Sometimes I crack myself up.

After about fifteen minutes I am stalling for time, the butterflies in my stomach leaving me unsettled. I know I started this game, but suddenly I am having second thoughts. Lost in my head, I hear a knock on the bathroom door. "Lexi, everything okay in there?"

Maybe Royce will take the lead from here.

CHAPTER SIXTY-FIVE

ROYCE

After Lexi surprised me in the shower, I had to get my head together. I have been doing everything in my power not to move too fast, but I think Lexi moved to the fast lane. I can see some hesitation in her eyes so I hand her the white hotel robe I placed in the bathroom for me. Grabbing a towel, I close the door behind me.

I sit on the edge of the bed in my towel waiting for Lexi to come out of the bathroom. I can hear her blow drying her hair, but after about fifteen minutes I knock on the door. She opens it looking like an angel. I am speechless. Seeing each other at bed time is nothing new, but there is something different about tonight. I kiss her, pick her up, and throw her on the bed. Tonight, I am claiming Lexi as mine. There will not be much sleeping tonight.

After the best night of my life with Lexi, I decide to let her sleep. I go to the coffee shop and grab some coffee and bagels. The closer I get to the lobby area I hear voice and moaning through the sound system.

What in the heck is going on? That sounds like Lexi and oh my god! That is me! Who in the hell would tape us and how did they know? Wait. I know who would do it, but how did he do it when he dosen't know where we are staying?

Barely holding my anger in, I walk over the front desk, "Excuse me, miss? Can you give me some information?" "Sir, if this is about the inappropriate media that is currently playing, we already issued out an official statement. Someone has hacked our system. We are unable to stop the audio at this time, but we have our techs working on it." "Do you know who hacked this system?" Just then my phone rings. "Hello," I answer. "How do you like the music playing in the lobby this morning?" Justin sneers.

"Well since it is of me, I don't like it. Some people don't like to share like others. I don't know how you know where we are, but one thing is for certain, you are going down."

I hang up on him, and then my phone rings again. This time it is Jaxson.

"What is up, bro?"

"Where are you? Lexi is freaking out. She woke up and you were not there. She thinks you ran out on her and are repulsed by her."

"What? You have got to be kidding me. I came down to get us breakfast, and found out Justin taped us having sex last night. Luckily it wasn't video but our passion is streaming through the speakers this morning in the lobby."

"You have got to be kidding me!"

"Nope, afraid not. Just get Lexi to your room and I will be there in a minute. I have to destroy this."

CHAPTER SIXTY-SIX

LEXI

After the best night of my life, I awake to an empty bed. I don't hear the water running, but I go to look in the bathroom for Royce. Hmm, not here. Where could he have gone? My mind starts wandering and I feel myself start to panic. Maybe I am not great at sex. . . maybe what Justin keeps telling me is true, but why would Royce keep going on and on about how beautiful I am? Besides, he woke me up two other times in the middle of the night to take me again and again. Where in the heck was he?

It isn't too much after nine in the morning, so I call over to Dakota and Jaxson's room to see if they know where Royce might be. They always seem to be in cahoots with each other.

"Hello" D says in her morning voice.

"Have you seen Royce? He is not here and he didn't leave a note. I am kind of freaking out. After last night, why would he leave me?" I express with a sad desperate tone.

"Why would he run away Lexi?"

"Because I am not good in bed. Finally, one thing Justin has been screaming at me is true because Royce and I had sex all throughout the night and now he is gone." I cry.

"He wouldn't just up and leave you, Lexi, even Jaxson says he is not the type to have a one night stand. Jaxson is calling him to see where his ass is at," Dakota says.

I can hear Jaxson on his phone in the back ground and it doesn't sound good. I know Royce had to come back to the room to get his stuff. I would see him again but I am worried I ruined our relationship. Finally, Jaxson hangs up and lets out a loud sigh that I know can't be good. They need to start letting me in. Did Justin show up? Is the contract canceled? I can fix anything, right? Time to find out what Royce told his brother.

"D, can you put Jaxson on the phone, please? I need to hear what Royce told him."

"Jaxson, what did Royce say?" I ask.

"Lexi, come to our room and we will discuss everything here," Jaxson replies.

"Jaxson, you are scaring me. Why can we not discuss it over the phone?"

"Lexi all I am going to say is it is not great and Royce said you need to get to our room now."

I guess it is a good thing that I had put sweatpants on before I called Dakota's phone.

I head down the hall to Jaxson and Dakota's room. Royce is already there when I arrive. "What is going on?" I ask, "Why is everyone looking at me like I am about ready to die today?"

"I have some bad news, baby girl. . ."

I held my hand up and cut him off, "I don't know if I want to hear this."

"Baby girl, just listen to me. Somehow last night what we did and everything we said has been recorded. I don't know how he did it, but he did. Let me see your cell phone." Royce demanded.

I hand my cell phone to him and he takes out the battery, but I guess he doesn't find what he is looking for, so he puts it back together and hands it back to me.

"What were you looking for?" I ask him.

"A listening device. Somehow Justin knew we left on a chartered jet last night. He must have called and pretended to be me and got our room number and had someone slip a listening device in, because when I went to go get us breakfast this morning, we were on the television in the lobby, the sound of us making love was what everyone was listening to while eating breakfast."

I hang my head in disbelief. How embarrassing. I am panicking, I don't know what to do. I don't want him to win. I think Royce is starting to read my thoughts. . . "He is not going to win. I am going to do everything in my power to protect you. Do you hear me?"

"Sorry to disappoint, but unless you have more money than God, there is no way anyone can protect me from Justin. His family is filthy rich and powerful. They make people disappear daily. This is my fight. I appreciate everything you have tried to do for me, nothing is going to stop him until I am dead or he is dead." I state dejectedly.

After my little speech, Royce and Jaxson exchange looks with each other like they are having their own little conversation between the two of them. I probably don't want to hear the outcome of this conversation because I know I probably won't be happy about it. I keep having this feeling they are keeping something from us and that silent look tells me my suspicions are true. They are hiding something and it is big. Now are they going to fess up about it or just keep it to themselves?

"What's with the look?" Dakota asks them.

"Umm. . ." Jaxson starts to mutter.

"Well. . ." Royce isn't doing much better.

I guess I am going to save them for now, so I quickly change the subject.

"Does anyone have any ideas on how to get me away

from that asshole who loves to make my life hell?"

"I think we should go with what we originally talked about. Let's keep it business as usual. If he shows his face, we call the cops on him for harassment, but from here on out, since we know what he is capable of, we will keep track of all encounters including this mornings.""Okay, well today we need to go make sure the set up and decorating are on track for the fundraiser tonight." I tell them. "I need to change, but I am not changing in our room."

"I will go and grab your suitcase for you. I will be right back."

CHAPTER SIXTY-SEVEN

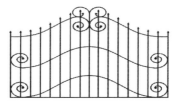

ROYCE

It is interesting that she says we need more money than God, because well we are up there with Oprah. I can't say anything, because right now is not the best time for her to digest that information on top of everything else happening.

I don't know how Justin managed having Lexi and I recorded in our room last night, but I intend to find out. I cannot believe Justin won't move on from Lexi.

After the girls are dressed and ready to go we head down and hail a cab for the ride to the aquarium. Jaxson and I did not plan on staying with the girls while they are putting on the final touches for the party, but after the events of the morning, we almost change our plans. i decide to have one of the security officers pose as a worker of the aquarium. I know they are going to head back to the hotel to change before the event tonight, so we will check in on them in a couple of hours. Jaxson and I have some emails we have to catch up on and we are going to do a video meeting as well. I also want to make sure all the extra security and cleaning crew we hired are up to speed on everything happening. I don't want anything ruining tonight. Jaxson and I decide to extend our trip a couple of days to do some sightseeing with the girls, and we are going to tell them after their party tonight.

After a couple hours of checking emails and having a video meeting I hear Jaxson's phone ring. "Hello, hey honey what's up?" Jaxson speaks into his phone.

"Hey Jaxson, Lexi and I are almost done can you and Royce head to our location and we will meet you out front."

"Yeah, sure that shouldn't be a problem we will leave right now."

"Great, see you in a few minutes then."

Jaxson and I head back to the aquarium to escort the girls to the hotel and get ready for tonight's fundraiser.

CHAPTER SIXTY-EIGHT

LEXI

It takes Dakota and I only about two hours to put the finishing touches for the party tonight. We are planning a fundraiser for the Chicago aquarium's program, Dream to Believe Always, where they host underprivileged children for a day. The kids get to learn all areas of the aquarium, whether it is the business side or taking care of the animals. They get to tour behind the scenes and they also are helpers for the day.

Dakota and I have only viewed the pictures of the foyer empty, but when we entered the building it is totally transformed by the hands of Party People International Designs, the company we hired to bring our vision for this fundraiser to life. As you enter the foyer, the lights are turned down with a light aqua back light. There is a soft see through lace draped from the columns to help add more height to the already massive area. Floor to ceiling windows capture the beauty of the aquarium itself. We have round circular tables set up to seat twelve guests.

The tables are covered with a simple light aqua tablecloth that has a white lace overlay. There are sand dollars and starfish placed throughout the tables. In the center of each table sits a glass fish bowl with lit floating candles. Green, blue, and clear rocks alternate throughout the fish bowls on the tables. The tables are set with white square plates and square glasses. I found these glasses in a thrift store and fell in love with them, I had to go to the manufacture to have enough for tonight's event. Sitting on top of the square plates is a menu of tonight's choices for dinner: Beef or chicken, mash potatoes, asparagus wrapped in bacon, and your choice of a red velvet, chocolate, or a vanilla cupcake with a star fish on top.

Off to the right of the dinner tables we have a dance floor set up with Christmas lights draped from the columns, which gives it a romantic atmosphere. At the back of the room we have a table set up with our silent auction items. We have a variety of items to be auctioned and baskets. The basket themes include: chocolate, movie lovers, a man's candy bouquet, airline tickets, a free year pass to the aquarium, and a huge jewelry basket.

When I finish my last task, I step back and take in the scene around me. I cannot believe tonight is here. What Dakota and I have worked so hard for. Please let tonight be successful.

I hear Dakota approach from behind me, "I think everything is ready for tonight!" she exclaims. "We should go and get ready. I have already called Jaxson."

CHAPTER SIXTY-NINE

ROYCE

When we get back to the hotel, Lexi refuses to get ready in our room. I can't say that I blame her after the morning's events. Lexi and Dakota barricade themselves in Dakota and Jaxson's room to beautify themselves. It only takes Jaxson and I about thirty minutes to get ready, while Lexi and Dakota take about two hours. I am afraid we were going to be late getting back.

Just as I get ready to lift my hand to knock on the bedroom door, Dakota flings it open and announces Lexi's presence. Lexi walks out in a strapless chiffon high-low dress that is white on the top of the dress and it cascaded down gradually getting darker in color until the bottom half of the skirt is black. She has it paired with a pair of silver high heel sandals that she had tied up her ankles with silver ribbon. There are also tassels hanging around her ankles. She looks amazing!"Wow! Lexi, you look sexy!"

"Thanks, you look pretty snazzy yourself."I am dressed

in a pair of black slacks with gray pinstripes and a gray shirt. It isn't much different than what I would wear to a business meeting.

Dakota is dressed in a short black dress with a scalloped hem line and a pair of red heels, which she has tied around her ankles almost like Lexi's, but Dakota's shoes don't have tassels hanging off them. Jaxson cannot keep his eyes off Dakota. I feel the same way about Lexi. Jaxson has on a red shirt along with a pair of black slacks. I secretly think they planned to match. Gag me! I don't know what to think about these two. They seem to be getting extremely serious in a small amount of time. I have no room to judge, but dang, I didn't try and sleep with Lexi the first night I met her.

After escorting the girls back to the aquarium for the fundraiser, Jaxson and I leave the girls to their party and we roam the aquarium grounds. We stay in constant contact with the extra security we hired. We don't want to get in the way of the girls doing their job, but we need them safe.

CHAPTER SEVENTY

LEXI

The night was a success, Dakota and I could not have been happier with the way everything had turned out. The clients are happy with how the evening flowed and the amount of money they raised. I know Royce and Jaxson are around here somewhere.

"Well, D, looks like we pulled off our first party without a hitch and the clients were ecstatic happy with our work." I marvel.

"You're right. I couldn't be happier. We just proved to ourselves that we can do this and be very successful in this profession. Time to let the social media world know we didn't fall flat on our butts." Dakota squeals.

"I wonder where the guys are. I thought they would have been back here by now. I told Royce we would be ready by 11pm. Let's walk out to the front to get some fresh air and see if we can find them."

Dakota nods her head in agreement and we proceed out to the front of the building. We turn to our left and I see the guys walking towards us on a trail down by the water. "Oh I see them! They are just down that trail." They are not close enough to hear, but the next thing I know I have this large piercing object being thrust into my back multiple times. I gasp for breath, and then I collapse on the sidewalk. Everything turns dark. The last thing I hear was a sneering laugh and Dakota screaming my name.

I have no idea what happened next, when I wake up I am in the arms of Royce and he is leaning over me shirtless because he is pressing his shirt anywhere on my wounds to try and stop the blood, but I am covered in it. I am trying to keep my eyes open, but the darkness is pulling me into it and can't hold on.

"Come on, baby girl, just take deep breaths. Help will be here soon, just stay with me," Royce whispers in my ear.

"I can't breathe. It hurts too bad to breathe." I whisper with shallow breaths. Royce leans in, he can hardly hear me.

"I know it hurts, but you got to stay with us, okay baby girl? Don't worry about anything else besides breathing and getting better." He is whispering in my ear. "I hear the ambulance. Don't close your eyes. Keep looking at me."

"Where are Dakota and Jaxson? What happened to Justin," I asked, breathlessly right before the paramedics reach me. Royce can't answer me, because they push him out of the way.

"Can I ride with her? She needs me to be with her." Royce asks?

"Only if you are family," the paramedic tells him.

"I am her husband," Royce says without missing a beat. Did I hear him, right? Did he just call me his wife or am I just hearing things?

"Okay, go sit in that jump seat right behind the driver. This way you are not in the way and we can still work on your wife," the paramedic explains to him.

"Jaxson, get Dakota to the hospital and I will meet you there. I am going to ride with Lexi to make sure she isn't alone and scared," Royce directs.

"No problem bro, take care of her. We have everything else under control. Justin won't be going anywhere anytime soon." Jaxson says with a gleam in his eye.

What did that look even mean? What happened to Justin while I was blacked out on the sidewalk?

Somehow while they are working on me in the ambulance, the way Royce and I are situated we can hold hands, and it is comforting to know he is with me.

"Mrs. James?" the paramedic asks me a question and I don't answer. "Mrs. James?" The paramedic continues.

Royce squeezed my hand, as if to say you need to answer the paramedic. "Yes," I say finally acknowledging him.

"What is your pain on a scale from one to ten?"

"I don't know. It just hurts, make the pain go away." I say in a very shallow breath voice. They have the huge full face oxygen mask on me. I want it off but Royce wouldn't let me.

"Baby girl, leave the mask on, it is helping you to breathe, just take breaths in and out. Focus on that and me, do not worry what anyone else is doing right now," Royce guides me.

At that moment that my world is closing in on itself. My body doesn't want to fight any longer to breathe, or stay with Royce. I am tired and I just want to sleep, but every time I close my eyes, Royce squeezes my hand to make sure I am not going to fall into the blackness that my body is calling me into.

"Baby girl, stay with me. We are almost there."

"So tired. . . I am so tired, Babe."

"I know, but hold out just a minute more. We are going to get you better. Do you hear me? Just one more minute until we get you the care you need," Royce reassures.

CHAPTER SEVENTY-ONE

ROYCE

Walking back up the trail from the river front I see the girls starting to walk towards us from the front of the building. I am scanning the area and nothing is out of place.

Dakota and Lexi turn a bit to wave at us, so we know that they have spotted us. I start to smile and wave back and then my heart is ripped out of my chest. I see Justin coming out of the blue and attacks Lexi. I scream, but I am still a good distance away. Jaxson who has always been faster than me runs and starts fighting with him, while I go to Lexi. I try to calm her down, and make her stay awake. I don't even know who called the ambulance and police, but I am grateful so all I have to worry about my baby girl.

I whisper encouraging words into her ear. I am frantically trying to get the bleeding to stop, but at the same time I keep trying to sooth. I need a medal, because that is some performance that I do not want to have to repeat.

I am not letting Lexi out of my sight, so I have to lie and tell the paramedics I am Lexi's husband. I know she needs me. And to tell the truth I need her more, I think. I need to know she is going to be okay and if I let her out of my sight, I don't want her to be scared. I don't want to panic that she might die. She is losing a lot of blood.

Lexi is rushed into surgery as soon as we arrived at the hospital to explore how much damage has been done and to repair it all, re-inflate her lung, and drain any fluid buildup. It takes about two and a half hours before anyone comes into the waiting room to talk to us.

"Family for Alexus James," the doctor announces.

"Yes, how is she? When can we see her?" I question as I jump up from my chair.

"She is in recovery. Surgery went well, and you will be able to see her in about an hour when we get her set up in her own room. The knife wounds missed all vital organs, but it did nick the spleen and we were able to repair that. Also, it hit a large chunk of the lung which was why she was having trouble breathing, but I don't foresee any problems with her recovery," the doctor explains.

"Thank you for all that you did." I say.

As soon as the doctor walks through the double doors, I hear Dakota ask me, "When did Lexi's last name become James?"

"Well I had to kind of lie so I could ride with her here to the hospital. I told the paramedic I was her husband, and well there you have it. I just haven't been able to correct them or say she kept her maiden name." I state smugly.

I stay with Lexi while she is in the hospital. I can't sleep. I sit and stare at Lexi to make sure she is still breathing. All night long she would moan and I would rub the back of her hand then she would relax, an hour later the process would repeat. This went on throughout the night. Finally it's morning and she starts to wake up, calling for me. At first she sound panicky, so I smile at her and continue to rub my thumb on the back of her hand.

Lexi is on oxygen, but at least she can say a few words before getting too tired.

"Hi." She smiles at me.

"Hey, baby girl." I respond with a huge smile.

I am not prepared for what comes out of her mouth next. "What happened to Justin?" she asks me and I frown.

I don't want to talk to Lexi about this, but I know she has a right to know. "When Jaxson and I saw what Justin did to you, Jaxson ran to Justin and I ran to you. Jaxson beat the crap out of Justin and held him until the police arrived. He got arrested and is currently in police custody. He is being charged with attempted murder, plus he has several other charges involving other ex girlfriends. The charges range from rape, stalking, and even a murder case. No more talk about Justin, though. He is locked up right now and he is not going to hurt you anymore. Now you need to get better," Royce tells Lexi.

"Okay, so can I ask you another question?"

"Sure, ask away."

I knew this was coming, but I was hoping it would be later and I had more time to think about how I will answer it.

"Um, did you say you were my husband to get into the ambulance?" She asks me.

"Yes. . . Yes, I did, and that is why your wrist band says your name is Alexus James. In my defense, I did it so you wouldn't ride alone, and I needed to make sure you were safe and made it to the hospital. It was a selfish reason, I know, but I couldn't let you be alone since I knew you were scared because, I know I was." I respond.

Lexi is speechless, and I decide it was time for her to rest. "Why don't you close your eyes and get some rest?"

CHAPTER SEVENTY-TWO

LEXI

When I wake up from my nap I noticed Royce is not there, but Dakota is sitting in the chair right next to my bed. "Dakota, where is Royce?"

"Well, it's nice to see you too. Royce has some phone calls he had to make so I thought I would sit with you and keep you company."

"Thank you, I have missed you."

"Lexi, our party was a huge success. We have been asked to do their next fundraiser in three months. Isn't that great?"

I am starting to get tired so I give Dakota a thumbs up as my hospital door was being pushed open. Dr. Matthews walked in. "Hey Lexi, I wanted to stop by and inform you that we are not going to discharge you for at least three more days. We are looking at Thursday. You need all the rest you can get. So, while you are here you need to sleep as much as possible."With that Dr Matthews turns and walks out of my room.

"Well, isn't she a ray of sunshine... Not." Dakota smirks.

Dakota is still sitting in the chair next to my bed when Royce returns to be by my side. Dakota greets him. "Hey Royce, Dr. Matthew's came by while you were gone and pretty much said Lexi isn't going to be released until Thursday. They want her to get as much rest as possible."

"Wow, I thought we would get her out of here and then get her a nurse out at the ranch. Well there isn't much we can do except for wait until they give us the okay to return to Montana."

First thing Thursday morning the nurse comes in to my room and has me sign all the discharge papers. Since Royce has been staying with me here at the hospital, Jaxon and Dakota packed all our stuff at the hotel and checked out of our room for us. We will be meeting them at the air strip where we will be flying out.

"Royce, I hope you and your brother don't lose too much business since you guys stayed in Chicago longer than you were expecting to."

"No, we checked in and everything is fine. Don't you worry about us. You still need to get a lot stronger and I expect you to rest on the flight back home."

CHAPTER SEVENTY-THREE

ROYCE

Lexi checks out of the hospital and then we head to meet Jaxon and Dakota at the air strip where we will be boarding our plane back to the ranch. I settle back on the king size bed so she can sleep while we are flying. She did not hesitate to go lie down. She is so tired, I practically had to carry her to the bed. I lie down with her, since I haven't gotten a lot of sleep while staying in the hospital, and I know she still has issues with being alone. While we both know Justin is being held without bail in Chicago, I still am not taking any chances where Lexi is concerned.

I still am not sure how we are going to tell Dakota and Lexi we are rich, but I am taking it one day at a time.

CHAPTER SEVENTY-FOUR

LEXI

Two months later in early fall

It has taken me two months to fully recover from all my injuries sustained in Chicago. I didn't get to celebrate Independence day because I was either in the hospital or recovering at Royce's house. But the good news is my car has been done since before we returned, but I have nowhere to go. Dakota informs me Jaxson has asked her to stay with him and she accepted. The only thing left for me to do is pack my stuff and head back to the Northwest. Royce has been busy with everything going on at the ranch, and we only see each other at bedtime. This has been going on for about five weeks. I decide I am probably getting in the way. Last night I tell him since I am well and not in anymore danger, I am going to going to be heading back to the Northwest to find another partner for my business since Dakota is staying in Montana with Jaxson.

The morning I am getting ready to leave, I open the front door and start out to where I have parked my car, but it is not parked out in front of the house. Where in the hell is my car? Royce better not be playing a trick on me because I am in no mood right now. I was hoping Royce would have stopped me and asked me to stay before I was done packing and ready load my car, but he didn't. I let my feelings for Royce get in the way of my judgment.

"Royce where is my car?" I yell as I am walking back into the house.

"Is it not out front where we parked it last night?"

"No, Royce. It isn't parked out front. Now tell me where my car is so I can get on the road." I continue to scream.

"What if I don't want you to leave the ranch?"

"What are you saying? Why would you wait until the day I am going to pack up and leave to tell me this?"

CHAPTER SEVENTY-FIVE

ROYCE

I have told Lexi before that I love her but I don't do it enough. I have loved her since I first laid eyes on her through the window of the diner, and every day I thank my dead parents she came into my life and now I have to keep her here.

She told me as soon as she was healed she was going to pack up and probably head back to Washington. Lexi found out that Dakota was going to be stay here on the ranch with Jaxson. I am happy for them, but I am being a chicken and not telling her how I feel about her.

The day Lexi decides she is going to pack up and leave, I turn into a child. I hide her car so she can't leave. First, I hadve to explain everything.

After hanging up the phone I hear a voice yelling. "Royce where is my car?"

Well here goes nothing.

"Hey I need to talk to you, I love you and I don't want you to leave. I have been keeping extra busy, so I wouldn't have to admit to myself that I want you to stay with me forever. I couldn't stand it when you were stabbed. If you ever get hurt again, I don't want to have to lie and tell them that you are my wife just so I can make sure you are not scared and all alone. I don't expect you to say it back because really I just sprang this on you but--"

Lexi cuts me off, "Will you just shut up for a minute? I know you love me just as you know that I love you, but I wanted to let you know from the first time you helped me up off the floor of the diner because of the asshole who we will keep nameless, I felt a spark that ran through the core of my body. I had to be near you. I had to touch you, and then you didn't run away when all those horrible things were yelled at me and even when he rammed your car to try and injure me but failed. You never faltered and you wanted to get to know me. You wanted to be with me, and for you to lie so you could ride with me in the ambulance, and to be able to stay with me and find out all the medical information that normally they wouldn't have told you, that tells me a lot." Lexi exhales.

"Please, stay with me. I don't ever want you to leave. Dakota is staying with Jaxson, so it is not like you would have to be alone and you two can still have your party planning business."

"Babe, I am staying. I want to see how this relationship plays out, without the fact that there has been a crazy man trying to derail us along the way."

"You're staying!" I exclaims.

"Yeah, I am staying. Now where is my car? I am not packing because I don't think I can stand not sharing a bed with you. I have come to love snuggling with you in your bed. And as soon as you're ready, I say we start making babies in that bed of yours."

"Babies? Don't you want to be married first before we start having babies?" I question.

"Well, big boy, are you going propose soon, because I am ready to have me some babies."

"You will just have to wait and see," I tease. "Come here and give me a kiss."

This feels right. Now, I must get through dinner, it probably will not be a pretty sight. Okay, so maybe at first we kept our wealth away from the girls only because we have been used and I think if we explain it that way to them, then they may understand. But they are both passionate people and I know this is going to hurt them. We should have told them after we ran the background checks on them. I never want to have any secrets again from my baby girl.

Well, I still have one secret and that is going to come out in the end as well since the ring is in my pocket, and I hope she says yes.

"How about we go to the diner and have some dinner with Dakota and Jaxson? Do you think they will let you back in since you probably won't fall down now?" I asked Lexi.

"Oh very funny, you and I both know how much stress my body was under. I am surprised I didn't get sick over everything. I guess I have you, Jaxson, and D to thank for that, since you did keep a lot of it away from me with deciding what would probably work best even, though I was a total child when I thought I needed to be involved."

"Baby girl, that is one of the reasons I fell in love with you, because you didn't want my help and you were very stubborn about it. Even though I won the arguments doesn't mean I was happy about it."

"Also I never got a hospital bill, and your brother didn't give me a bill for fixing my car. Do you happen to know whatever happened with that?" Lexi questions, her eye brow raised.

"Uh, your hospital bill? Well, it's funny you should mention that. I was told that it was paid in full and that there was no bill."

"What do you mean there was no bill? It's a hospital. They bill you for blowing your nose on a tissue, let alone a surgery and a five or six day stay. Plus, I didn't have insurance because I was just kicked off my parents plan when I graduated college. Royce, I know you are hiding something from me. I have been patient enough, please let me in and tell me what the big secrete is that I saved you and Jaxson from in Chicago."

"You will find out tonight at dinner. Jaxson and I are planning on talking to you and Dakota together. Can you hold off just a little bit longer?"

"All right fine, since you have a plan I will not derail it. I will wait a little bit longer, but I will know before this day is over, got it?"

"Yes dear, I got it and you will know by the end of today," I mimic.

CHAPTER SEVENTY-SIX

LEXI

This has been the longest day waiting around the ranch until dinner tonight, but I told Royce that I would let him tell me with his brother, and it wouldn't be fair to Dakota if I knew before she did. To keep busy, I go on a stroll along the ranch like I did when I was trapped here. Now that I am free to roam and leave when I pretty much want to, I love being on the ranch. It doesn't feel like a prison sentence anymore.

It is finally time to go to dinner and I want to dress nicely. I call and talked to Dakota earlier in the day and we decide to treat this as a date night. So, I wear a nice summer maxi dress with sandals, and I never go anywhere without my Maui Jim sunglasses and my Dooney and Bourke purse as my accessories.

When we all arrive at the diner, we decided to just take Royce's Range Rover. The guys sit up front, and D and I sat in the back. We are letting the guys talk quietly up front so they can make a game plan. We are having a blast just talking, because Dakota and I can talk for hours upon hours about nothing and laughing at the littlest things. That is why we had chosen to drive across the country. Never a dull moment with her.

Finally reaching the diner, we are able to grab what is becoming our regular booth, a table in the very back corner, because the guys don't want to be overheard while we are having our conversation. We all quickly order our drinks and meals to make sure that our table doesn't get much interruption, which we politely informed the waitress. She readily agrees and just brings us our drinks and tells us that our food will be ready in about twenty-five minutes, and that is when she will be back to check on us and bring our dinners to us.

The time was upon us and both Jaxson and Royce are looking very sick with worry. I am guessing whatever they have to tell us normally doesn't go over very well, but I am willing to hear them out and only talk when it was my time to say something in the conversation.

"Okay girls, we both asked you to join us for dinner because we have some interesting news to share with you." Jaxson starts.

"Normally this is not a huge discussion because the people in this town know our 'secret', but since you ladies came from out of town, this is something that we don't like to talk about," Royce continues.

"What Royce is trying to say is that our family is pretty well off in the finance department."

"Jaxson" I say, "I knew you were pretty well off or that you do really well in business. This is not new to Dakota and I."

"Yes, you two have deducted that we are well off by the vehicles we drive, or the houses that we live in but, what you do not realize is that the plane that we took to Chicago, well, that is our plane. It has been in my family for years. So, we kind of lied, but we like to think of it as stretching the truth a little bit. If we would have come out and said that this is our plane you would have never agreed to do it, as it was you guys who did not want to use the plane, which we respect. We do not like to flaunt our wealth, but sometimes it is necessary." Jaxson states as a matter-of-factly.

"So, is this why I haven't gotten any bills from anything? No food checks, my hospital bill, having my car fixed for free, and the list could go on forever." I ask.

Dakota just stays quiet. I think she was trying to digest everything, but I know something is bothering her. Finally, she speaks up. "How much money are you guys actually worth?" She continues to babble on. "I know it is not my place to ask, but you guys are making such a huge deal out of it. I understand you didn't want to tell us in the beginning because you didn't want us to like you for just your money, but we are not some bimbos who throws themselves at the rich people of the world," Dakota huffs.

"Did you think I was only after someone with money? Because, if you did, then I should just pack up my stuff right now and leave. Justin was the one who came after me. Yes, he had money, but I always wanted to work hard for my money. I didn't want to ride on the coattails of my husband. It would be great if I didn't have to work so I could one day stay home with the children that I bare, but I am not going to be a gold digger," I yell.

I am starting to get upset. I have just lost my appetite, so I stand and walked out of the diner. I throw a couple of bucks on the table to cover my part of the meal, so the guys don't think I am mooching off them. I end up just walking around town to let off some steam. I will have to have a ride back to the ranch, where I plan to pack my stuff and head out. I am not going to stay around here and have Royce think that I only want him for his money. My mamma didn't raise a fool.

CHAPTER SEVENTY-SEVEN

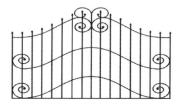

ROYCE

Dinner didn't go as planned, Nervously I explained to Lexi our wealth and why we didn't tell them about it – and why we went so far as to even lie about the plane.

Both Lexi and Dakota are in shock about us keeping our wealth a secret. Lexi then shoots up and bolts out of the diner. She just paces outside the front door. I go to comfort her, but I am probably the last person she wants to see. I go anyway, and get a mouthful thrown into my face. I love that my Lexi is spitfire.

"Lexi. Lexi, please stop I want to talk to you," I say holding my arms out as I am stalking towards Lexi.

"Royce, just leave me alone! I am waiting until we go back to the ranch and then I am getting my bags and leaving like I had planned on doing this morning before you hid my car." Lexi screams.

"You are not leaving the ranch Lexi, not like this. I love you."

"You don't love me! If you loved me at all, you wouldn't have kept this from me or assumed I would only like you for your money!" she continues to yell. "Royce apparently you don't know me, because you would know that I work for everything I have. My car is the only thing my parents ever gave me that was not something I needed to have, and the reason they gave it to me was because they were proud of me for graduating college."

"Lexi, it is not that I didn't trust you. I don't talk about my wealth. We have a mix of old money and new money due to the garage and what we have added to our ranch. I think most of the time, I just want to be a real person who doesn't have to worry all the time over who is trying to get to me because of my money. That is why I didn't tell you."

"That still doesn't explain why you didn't tell us sooner if you already knew you loved me, you crazy ranch man."

"Really, it never came up, and how do you start a conversation by saying 'oh by the way I am a billionaire a couple of times over'?"

"Fine I get it, I really do, but it still hurts. I feel like you are going to always look at me like I am a money hungry bimbo," Lexi whines.

"Baby girl, I would never look at you like a money hungry bimbo. You are always going to be my stubborn baby girl."

Fine, but can you take me home and make love to me please?"

"I will only make love to you if you. . ."

I want to make love to Lexi so bad it hurts, but the smart spitfire has made me play my last ace up my sleeve. I get down on one knee and say, "Alexus will you do me the honor of becoming my wife?"

CHAPTER SEVENTY-EIGHT

LEXI

What? I was only joking around. He is on his knee and he is waiting for my answer. He just accused me in not so many words that he maybe thought that I was only after him for his money, and I just put him in his place. He is simply staring at me. I guess I should give him an answer but it has only been weeks. Are we really in love or in lust with each other? I know I can't sleep without him next to me and in his arms. He keeps the nightmares I have away and has protected me from the first moment he picked me up off the floor.

Tears are streaming down my face. "Yes, yes, yes, I will marry you. I will still be working and planning parties with Dakota, which means we will be going to many different cities just like we did in Chicago."

"That's fine Lexi, because I will be traveling with you. I don't want any other man trying to pick you up. I will be your security built into the company. The ranch is operating like a well-oiled engine."

"Well then, I can't wait to be your wife Mr. James."

"Me neither. I can't wait to be your husband."

"You two make us sick." Dakota and Jaxson both say.

"You two are just jealous of Lexi and I," Royce mocks.

"Nope, not in your dreams, big brother, because Dakota also agreed to be my wife."

"Well, it looks like the four of us need to celebrate." I say.

"Well how do you suggest we do that?" Dakota questioned?

"Road trip!" I squeal.

"Where do you want to go?" Royce asks me.

"I was thinking of going to Las Vegas. I hear they have lots of great shows and maybe I want to get married by Elvis?"

"Elvis, really?" Royce asks. "Jaxson it has been awhile since we made it out to Vegas. . . Let's do it."

I just can't believe it, I was ready to head back to my parents home in Washington and he pulls this. I shake my head in disbelief, this doesn't happen to me. We walk back into the diner so we can finish all the talking and eating that the boys had planed for us. "I should call my sister in Oregon and see if she wants to go with us. I haven't seen her in almost six years it would be fun to have her come with us. I want you to meet her" I say as he fog and tense moment that was a few moments before now reflects peace and calmness, I would even say there is a hopeful and optimistic vibe coming off the guys.

I am sitting next to the best guy in the world staring into the gorgeous ring that now sits on my finger. Royce is talking to his brother Jaxson. What they are talking about I have not one iota of a clue. I am still in the haze of Royce just proposed to me. I am trying to figure out if he did it so I wouldn't leave or if he really meant it. I know how I feel about him, it is written all over my face. Royce tends to keep his feelings locked to where no one knows what he is really thinking. I keep thinking 'why would he want me. I am too fat, I am not pretty enough. ' Royce is drop dead gorgeous. A smile to die for. I would even go as far as saying Royce is just as gorgeous and the ring he gave me when he proposed a few minutes ago. A ring that I can not take my eyes off of. It is a white gold band with it looks to me like it is two-point-five carets in the center stone, in a princess cut shape. It also has a cluster of diamonds weighing a half caret on each side. I am so happy to have Royce wanting to call me his.

I was starting to let my guard down, I knew that Justin wasn't going to come after me. He was locked up and couldn't touch me any more. Or at least that is what I thought until the lights go out in the diner. I hear screams of shock. I immediately tense and I feel Royce get out of the booth, at the same time I hear Jaxson doing the same. These James men should be twins because they think and act like it. Anyway, my heart rate has skyrocket, and my breathing betrays me. I feel someone next to me but because I can't see who it is, I do have a feeling I know who it is because the hairs on my arms and on my neck is standing tall. I am trying to inch away from whoever it is with no luck. I am freaking out inside because I need to see who is creeping me out. It could be Justin himself or he could have brought Steve again to do some dirty work. Either way both men are creepy and very dangerous.

My hearing senses has heightened ten fold, I can hear everything that is going on but cannot see who it involves and I am worried that I know who is going to get hurt. I am just praying quietly that Royce and Jaxson will be alright. I don't want anyone to get hurt but my feeling of calm is gone. I will never be safe again. I need to get away from Royce, Jaxson, and Dakota. I can't drag my family into this, I am just going to have to figure out a way to leave my friends and family. I need to take care of this on my own. Damn him. Justin is wrecking my life one word and action at a time. Whether he has hired someone to come get me or if he has come back to get me himself.

CHAPTER SEVENTY-NINE

ROYCE

I had the women I loved sitting next to me while I was talking to my brother. I was trying to explain to him that I was wrong and we should not have waited to tell our women everything about us. Lexi was right, I might have had one or two thoughts about maybe they wanted our money. I am man enough to say when I was wrong and that is what I was doing. Then the lights in the diner go out.

I didn't think I just got out of the booth and went to see what was going on. I also wanted to make sure the back of generator was working. The lights should have come back on quickly because the generators would kick in. As soon as I get out of the booth I feel my brother right next to me. We are not going to let anyone get hurt. It is a good thing that Jaxson and I eat here quite a bit because we know the layout better than the back of our hands. So we are slowly making our way to the back where the generator is located. This is our town. People think our town is an easy target because we don't have police near by. We have to rely on the state cops and they aren't always able to be here. So Jaxson and I try and keep the peace as much as possible. We have friends who are like the unofficial deputies and that is who we call. If it is bigger than that then we call the state police in.

Once outside we notice that it was unplugged. We look at each other. This is not going to be good, but we have a good suspicion that this was intentional. I don't know how we knew but we knew, this makes us run back into the brightly lit diner, and over to our booth. You know the one is the back corner where we always end up. I think the diner has this reserved for us when ever we come in. The look on Lexi's face tells me more than enough to know.

"Lexi, baby what happened?" I demand more forcefully that I originally intend.

Dakota jumps to Lexi's defense. "Royce nothing happened. I didn't feel anyone come to our booth, I didn't hear any commotion as if anyone came over. Just the normal scared screams of the lights going out."

"Thank you Dakota, but by the look on Lexi's face something happened. One thing I came to realize is that you can not under-estimate Justin or his family."

In the smallest voice I have ever heard this is what Lexi told us. "I think he was here. He had to have been super quiet because my hearing was heightened since I couldn't see anything. He had to have sit on the edge of the booth but still super close to me, the only way I know it was him was because the hair on my arms and on my neck stood tall."

As soon as she told me that, a bad feeling was growing in the pit of my stomach. I could feel a huge shift in Lexi. Her demeanor changed. She was going to crawl inside of herself. I didn't want to believe it. Well, she had one thing coming to her. I loved her too damn much for her to run. She doesn't have to take this all on her own. Jaxson and I spoke at great lengths about this situation and we were going to protect our women. Come hell or high water we will not let anything happen to our women.

"I think its a good time to head back to the ranch. You need to call your sister and tell her the great news. Maybe we could do New Years with her or Christmas."I suggest as we get into the car.

"That sounds like a good idea." Lexi says in a small voice. I know she is starting to retreat. But, I want to try and keep her from retreating too much.

CHAPTER EIGHTY

LEXI

We get back from dinner at the diner, I didn't eat much. I am just too numb to do anything. Royce is looking at me like I am broken, and you know what? I am broken. I finally realize what the guys were talking about the last time we were up against Justin. I need to get away before anyone gets hurt. I would not be able to live with myself if the people I love get hurt. Its time my tired and broken body and spirit goes up to take a bath and come up with a plan.

"Royce, I am going to take a bath and then lay down. I am not feeling well."

"Baby I can come keep you company."

"No, I just want to be alone for a bit. Don't worry I am fine."

"Your not fine. Don't push me away. I love you and want to help."

"I am not pushing you away. I just need a few moments to myself." When in fact I am trying to push him away. He doesn't need all this extra stress that comes along in the form of Justin or the Kramers. This is my problem, which I have stated over and over again. I know Royce means well but I don't want to get him or his brother killed. Jaxson can watch over Dakota and Royce will be fine in the long run. He actually might be relieved that I am going to be gone. This was a great dream while it lasted.

A plan forms while I am in the tub. I am going to go to town while Royce is busy with ranch work. I will get questioned by the guards because I am sure Royce is going to inform them that I am not to leave without anyone. But I will make up an appointment or some other business that I have to go to. I know a couple people have come up to me and ask if I could help with planning the town festival. I hadn't wanted to get involved because I didn't think I was staying. Well now I know I am not staying but I won't let the security guards know that. It is time to relax and just get through the night without giving anything way to Royce. I swear he is a human lie detector.

"Honey, are you okay in there?" I hear Royce on the other side of the door.

Here goes nothing. "Yes I am fine. You can come and see for yourself if you don't believe me."

"I didn't want to smother you. If you want some company then I will be more than happy to come in there, even if it is to just wash your back." He expresses.

"I want you to come in, I just want you to hold me. So get in here fast." I say evenly. I can't let him in on my thoughts about the whole situation. Is Justin back is he going to come after me until he finally kills me? Too many emotions to try and sort anything out.

"What's going on in your head? You are not acting like yourself." Royce whispers in my ear in a concerning matter.

"Nothing much happening in my head." I act nonchalantly. Boy, maybe my plan will work and even though I hate lying this is going to be the best in the long run. I just know it. I continue with a lame excuse I know this and I bet he does too, but it is worth a shot. "I guess the lights going out spooked me more than I originally thought."

"You have nothing to worry about. You and Dakota are safe here, Jaxson and I can and will protect you. So don't you forget it. Got it?" He questions with a kiss to my forehead.

"Yeah I get it." I sigh. Maybe my idea to run is not a good one. Who am I kidding. I am not worth all the trouble. Love can not fix this. Love will only get you killed. Royce and his brother didn't get that memo. I mean look at what happened to his parents. Yeah I know they can't prove it but now knowing how dangerous Justin and the rest of his family is like. I shiver at the thought.

Royce grabs me closer to his chest and sweetly asks, "are you cold?"

"No" I sigh as I cling to him harder.

"I am not taking any chances, let's get you out of this tub and into the nice warm bed. I don't want you sick."

If being sick was the least of my worries right now but I readily agree. "Sounds good. I am exhausted from the highs and lows of the day." Knowing that in the morning I will leave my newly acquired new engagement ring and a note, telling him that even though I love him and appreciate everything he and his brother have done for me. But I can't let it keep going like this. I don't want him killed and ask him to not contact me. I need to make a clean break and I need to save his life.

Dakota will understand and she is happy with Jaxson. She will be sad and mad with me leaving like this but only because I probably won't see her again. I hope that her and Jaxson get married and live the life she deserves.

In the morning I wait until Royce goes to do his morning work, then I mike my break. I am not ready but at the same time I know that I have to do this. Time to put my plan into motion.

CHAPTER EIGHTY-ONE

LEXI

I know Lexi was having a hard time after the blackout at the diner. It was killing me that she wasn't opening up to me. How can I protect her if I don't know what is going on. I held her all night and she slept like crap. I don't know if she was having nightmares or if she was still on edge. All I know is that this needs to stop. She needs me to love and protect her. I was having nightmares all on my own when the alarm goes off.

A blaring noise is yelling at me to get out of bed, but this morning I didn't want to leave Lexi to tend to the animals. I thought this is why I had ranch hands who I paid very well. I sigh cause I know I want to be out there with them, and a ranch never stops or takes a day off. So grudgingly I went to work, knowing that I was going to finish as fast as my human body can move. All throughout my chores I had a feeling that something bad was going to happen. Call me paranoid or something but I call it being cautious. I make a call to the security building asking if anything out of the ordinary happened overnight. Plus I semi demanded to know if Lexi leaves the ranch and where she is going. I did end the phone call with a polite thanks. Then hung up on them.

After my call it eased my nerves a bit but not all the way. Look I am starting to get a good read on Lexi and so I know she is going to think the I am not worth it or its not my battle. Blah, Blah, Blah. Well I guess I am going to have to remind her until she gets it. My phone rings.

As I pull out my phone and notice its the security shack. It really isn't a shack, but that is what we nicknamed it.

"Hello." I demand in the why the hell are you calling me voice.

"Um, I just wanted to let you know Lexi just left the ranch." Stu my number one guard stuttered.

"Where did she go?" I am trying to reign it in but it is difficult. I really shouldn't have to ask these questions. They should just supply the information for me.

"She told us that she was going to town for a meeting about the town festival. I knew that couldn't be be right but we let her go anyways."

"You what!" Now I am screaming.

"Well we couldn't tell her no or stop her. You told us she was free to come and go as she pleases as long as we know where she is heading." Stu reminded me.

"You guys had better know where she was really going so I can go and get her. If you don't then I suggest you find her QUICKLY!" Enough with being nice, I am no yelling at everyone because she left. I run into our house it's not just mine anymore. Let's face it, it was hers just as much the first night she slept in my bed. I run into our bedroom and sure enough her suitcase is gone. I don't have time to sit around, I need to act now and go get my Lexi, my baby girl. The women who I am supposed to marry. I quickly dial Jaxson, he will know what to do in this situation. He is the one who keeps a level head where as I normally run around with my head cut off. But I know if the situation was reversed then I would be the one who probably had the calm head.

"Jaxson, Lexi is gone."

"What are you talking about?" The way he said it sounded like he thought I was joking, like she would be coming through the front door with milk.

"Her suitcase is gone and the shack said she gave them a lame excuse for leaving. They let her go without seeing if it was okay. Can you believe that?

"Royce you can't chain her to the ranch."

"Watch me." I am now officially off my rocker. More so than when Justin attacked her on the sidewalk in Chicago.

"Calm the hell down dude. I will have Dakota call her and see if she can get anything out of her. Come over and we will figure this out."

CHAPTER EIGHTY-TWO

LEXI

I can't believe the guards fell for what I told them. He gave me a blank look. It was the kind of look that said he didn't believe me but they let me go anyway. Which makes me think that they called Royce to inform him of my leaving. Sorry dude, better you than me anyway. The ringing of my phone scares the crap out of me. I look at the caller id on the dash board and I really don't want to answer it but it's D and I always take her calls.

Hey D." I say in my over cherry voice, and without missing a beat she says.

"Cut the crap. Where are you?" It is now that it clicks that I keep forgetting that Royce is super close with his brother, they tell each other everything. Something I have no clue about since my sister and I are not close. Then I keep forgetting that Jaxson always talks to D since she would know me the best. Now I am starting to doubt my best laid plan that took me all of twenty minutes to form.

"What do you mean where am I? I went to one of those

festival meetings that they town has been harping us to do."

"Well Royce knows otherwise. He knows your running the guys in the guard shack saw your missing suitcase. He is crushed. So this is the last time I am going to ask. Where did you go?"

I am sighing in defeat. "I don't know where I am going. In fact I am surprised to have cell service." Dakota is starting to settle down a bit, "why are you running? Can you at least tell me that?"

I am starting to rethink this tell my best friend everything. But sadly my mouth doesn't listen to my brain. Especially since Dakota is more than a best friend. She is my sister. "I have a good hunch and gut feeling that Justin is back or he has hired someone to come after me. I don't want anyone to get hurt and he is never going to stop. I know that now. I am not worth someone that I love getting hurt or worse killed."

"No one is going to be hurt."

"Well Dakota I am not taking that chance."

"It's not a risk, no one is going to get hurt." Its at this moment a car is coming up on me very fast. So fast in fact if they don't pass me in the next second or two I will be having a very bad day. It is at this moment that my brain forgets that I am still on the phone with Dakota, and I am talking out loud to what I think is an empty car. "Come on dude just pass me already."

"Lexi." Oh crap I am still on the phone, D continues "what are you talking about?"

I give up. "There is a car right up on my butt and it has no plans of getting off my back end, or going around me."

"Do you recognize the car?"

"Why would I recognize the car?" Answering a question is not one of my finer qualities but at this point who cares?

"I don't know I thought it might be Justin or something."

I look into the rear view mirror, and I see the eyes of a person I will never forget. Okay Lexi stay cool. You can not let on that Justin is behind you and he is not alone.

But before I can get anything out, I get a love tap on my back bumper. I look up and he is motioning me to pull over. Not so fast, I am not pulling over in the middle of no-where, I might have gullible before but today is a new day. So I keep driving and apparently in Justin's mind that was the wrong thing to do.

"Not today Justin." I say and I hear an audible sound that didn't come from me. Oh crap that's right I am on Bluetooth in my car and Dakota heard everything that just came out of my mouth. Ops.

"Did you just say Justin's name?"

"How important is the truth in this situation?"

"Don't start now. You better tell me the truth!"

"Yes, I said Justin's name. You guys don't need to worry about me. As long as I stay away you will have a happy life with Jaxson, Royce will find another lover and I will hopefully get my chance to kill Justin."

"Oh and how pray-tell do you plan to do that?" I hear Dakota say sarcastically.

"I don't know yet. Just tell Royce that I love him and I want him to be happy with and without me."

"You kind have done that yourself."

"Thanks for the heads up about being on speaker, I can't tell the difference since I am using the hands free feature."

"This is not a laughing matter."

"I didn't say it was. Wait why do I hear rustling in the back ground?"

"No reason I am just walking through the house. I got to go." She hung up on me. Well at least one thing is for sure. I didn't say he wasn't alone in the car. I hope to keep that little bit of information to the grave.

CHAPTER EIGHTY-THREE

ROYCE

After I talked to my brother I ran to his house. I got there right as Dakota was calling Lexi. Yes, I made it in record time. I gesture to see if she would put it on speaker phone so I could hear it as well. I almost gave away the fact that I was hearing everything. I was coming unglued with each passing second because she was getting farther and farther away from me and she wasn't giving us any help to finding her.

There were a couple of times I was biting my tongue or cheek while making fists with my hands. I couldn't take much more than this, and then she says the one man's name who I would more than willing go to prison for killing him.

I turned around almost grabbed the phone but instead I ran as quickly and quietly as I knew how to out of that room. As I reached my Range Rover Jaxson grabs my shoulder to stop me.

"Let me go." I am so angry flamers were going to start

shooting our my ears.

"Stop Royce. Let me call a few of our buddies so we can track her cell phone. It will be a lot faster than driving all over the state of Montana blind."

"It will take too long. You heard for yourself that she is willing to sacrifice herself so no one else gets hurt."

"Take a breath. Le me drive and you start tracking her cell. I know Jaxson is right but I just want her back in bed with me. That Bastard and his family dead. I climb into the passenger seat while I hear Jaxson finishing his call. I hear him finish his call with a thanks man I owe you one. In reality it is I who owes him one not my brother. I will deal with that later.

Jaxson's phone pings with a text message. "Let's go we have her location." Jaxson pulls out of the ranch and hits the road faster than any normal human being should be driving. I am grateful and terrified at the same time. "Dude can you please slow down a bit. I know I want to get to Lexi as soon as we can but I also want to be in one piece."

"Sorry. I just want her safe as well, she has already become a sister to me. She is our family and you would do the same in regards to Dakota." Jaxson says as he nods his head towards the back seat. .

I hadn't realized that she jumped in the back. I need to refocus myself so I don't get anyone killed.

I slightly turn towards the back so I can look at Dakota. "He's right D, if the rolls were reversed I would be driving like a bat out of hell so he could save the day."

"Thanks Royce, that means a lot to me." Dakota sniffs as to try and hide the fact she might be crying.

Okay everyone hold on I am cutting though this field and we should be a couple miles away from her. We are lucky in the fact that she didn't make it very far. ' Jaxson informs us. Then Dakota asks, "how are we going to get her to stop and pull over?"

She has a very valid point. Then the best idea came to me.

"Dakota I need you to call her back and use the speaker phone so we can all hear, but instead of you talking to her I am going to talk instead."

"Is that a great idea? This might spook her more than she already is." Jaxson throws his two cents in.

"Look its the best and only idea I have on short notice. I am going to ask her to pull over with the doors and windows locked. Jaxson and I will handle Justin if he is still around. So Dakota you stay put with the windows and doors locked as well." I glance down at the GPS and she is just up ahead. Finally I can see her car, it looks like Justin decided not to chase her. That can't be good, that means he must be hiding somewhere to ambush us like before in Chicago. I can't think like that now, I need to get to my baby girl.

"Okay Dakota make the call, here goes nothing."

CHAPTER EIGHTY-FOUR

LEXI

I glance in my rear view mirror and notice no one is behind me. A huge sigh of relief escapes me. All of the sudden my phone is ringing, and again I jump out of my skin cause I am literally so scared that I have tears running down my face. I answer with a shaky "hello?" My fear being Justin coming through yelling at me to do as he wants. What I hear is "Baby girl" very hesitantly.

"Royce why are you calling me. Didn't you get my message from Dakota?"

"Baby, you need to pull off to the side of the road. Your crying so hard I don't know how your able to see to drive." Sniffle, sniffle, sniffle.

"How do you know I am driving?"

"Baby, look in your mirrors. Jaxson is driving my car. Pull over, it isn't safe for you to be driving like this."

I am crying, coughing, and laughing all at the same time. Royce is right but it really isn't safe for me to drive like this, but I also wanted to get away from my friends and family so they didn't get hurt.

"Lexi, with the silence on this phone conversation that you are probably thinking that I am right, but you are being stubborn. Look I don't see Justin around. Pull over and stop on the side of the road. Jaxson and I will come to you and then I am driving you home."

"Okay." Hick-up, sniffle. I start to slow down and veer over to the shoulder. I want to get out and run to Royce and not let go. But fear is holding me back. Fear that Justin is going to jump out and grab me, before Royce can get to me. Fear that I am too weak for Royce and my self worth is not going to be enough to keep him satisfied. So as the car comes to a stop, my mind is painting the picture that I am running to Royce, and wrapping my arms around him and not letting go. What I really end up doing is grip the steering wheel sobbing. Royce opens the door and has to pry my hands off the wheel, unbuckle my seat belt and drag me into this arms. It feels like heaven and I am never running from him again. "Baby girl, shh your okay." Sob, sob, sob. "Shh baby girl, I've got you. Come on let's get you back into your car and we can get home."

He picks me up like I weigh nothing and runs around the car to the passenger side. He gently puts me in and buckles my seat belt and kisses my forehead. I officially feel like a little child. Royce goes back to the drivers side, tells Jaxson something and give a quick brotherly hug. Before he gets in the car he watches his brother go to his range rover. It is weird to watch but both brothers get into the cars at the same time worrying about the other getting hurt. It is almost like they practiced this.

Royce starts the car and flips a U-turn and speeds away with Jaxson and Dakota on his heels. I know I should try and make conversation, but anything that comes out of my mouth is not going to sound good. It will sound weak, childish, and maybe even excuses. Royce won't understand my reasoning, he will probably think that they are stupid. Yes, I know he can protect me but I don't want him to feel obligated. I mean we barely know each other. Since day one he has been my knight and shining armor. In my mind that makes him feel obligated, he doesn't like the fact I had a rough background with men that is all this is. It has to be.

CHAPTER EIGHTY-FIVE

ROYCE

I want to tell Lexi how scared I was, how I lost it when she was gone. That is one the thing that she doesn't need. I don't know what is going on in her mind but she is acting like she did in the beginning all those weeks ago. I don't want her to retreat back into believing everything that Justin has spewed into her those four years they were together. Emotional abuse is just as much a problem as physical abuse. They are both abuse. One you can see and cover with make-up, the other you can cover as if nothing is wrong while all the while they are breaking on the inside.

"Lexi, sweetie are you okay?" I am very hesitant in asking but I can't take the silence any longer.

A long sigh from other side of the car is what I hear and then "yeah, I am okay I guess." She guesses? That is not going to cut it. I need her to open up and tell me what is really going on. Why she left and ran? Before I could get her to talk to me more the phone in her car rang.

"Hello?"

"Bro, we are being followed. There are two people in the car behind me."

"Do you recognize the people in the car?"

There is a pause on the other end of this conversation and I hear Dakota say Justin and Steve. Who is Steve?

"Who is Steve?"

"You remember, the dude that grabbed Lexi at the bar and we tied him up in the back alley."

"Why would he be with Justin?" Just then my stomach dropped. I need to get Lexi to the ranch and then we need to figure out what we are going to do. I look over to her and she doesn't seem very surprised that they are behind us.

"Just head to the ranch, we are going to split up and they can only follow one of us. Luckily we drive the same car so we might be able to confuse them." I tell Jaxson.

"Baby girl. Look at me. We are going to fix this. You are not going to have to live in fear."

Oh that struck a cord with her because she is now spewing venom at me. "For once in your life don't try and be the hero, you don't have to deal with him. This is my battle. I am not worth all this trouble. You don't deserve this."

"What in the hell do you mean you are not worth this? Huh? I would like you to enlighten me." I am so angry at hearing her talk about herself in that way.

"Royce if no one in my family ever cared to help out with protecting me instead of their image in the social circle then I don't expect you to protect me. Don't start with I love you and therefore you are responsible."

"Well just because you had to grow up alone and not have anyone there, doesn't mean I am going to do the same thing. My love doesn't doesn't come with strings. So if you think leaving will solve these problems and you can deal with this on your own. Let me tell you something, I will always come for you and protect you because you are worth it. Don't doubt me or my love for you. I am going to take care of you."

Well that made her quiet down. Maybe I was a little hard on her but she has got to stop running. I am just so mad that she thinks that she has to do everything herself. Have I not shown how much she means to me? I need to figure out what I need to do better to show her. The ranch as been running more smoothly so maybe I can pull back a bit and let the ranch hands take on more of the responsibility. I am going to have to talk to Jaxson about that. I know he has been keeping Dakota near him. I need to be doing the same thing and not just keep her hostage on the ranch. We are not going to be afraid of Justin or his goons. As for right now I am just going to let her rest.

CHAPTER EIGHTY-SIX

LEXI

Royce?" I don't know what I am going to say to him. Is I'm sorry enough? I mean, how do I tell him that I love him and his love should be enough, but my parents claimed that they loved me and they never paid much attention to me. They said they were proud that I graduated high school early, me I just think they were more happy that I was leaving the house and then they wouldn't have to worry if I would say or act and do something to tarnish the image of what they created.

"Yeah, baby girl?" He responds.

Well here goes nothing. "I" was all I could get out. So I just said, "never mind." It was at that moment that we returned to the ranch. I love seeing the gates, I really do feel at peace when I am on the ranch. I just love it here. When we return, I know this is where I want to be. I will try to get over my self doubts but its pretty hard. I once heard a lady talk about how everyone always made small snide comments about her weight her whole life. It was during freshman week where they bring in different people to give the income freshman seminars about life while in college and then also what might happen after college. Well this lady whose name is Carol was talking about respect and self image, she was telling us all these different stories in her life and because of her self image and what she saw of herself and not what others saw, she wished she was able to voice how all that made her feel. So as Carol kept telling all these stories her self image was harmed her whole life. She tried not to let what others get her down that is all she heard in her head. So while she was in High school she went to this wedding with her mom, and she recounted to my freshman class that her mom would tell her that people would come up and speak to her mom saying how pretty she was but if she just lost the weight she would be that much more pretty. I don't remember the whole story but the part that hits me every time is that her mom never stood up for her. So if her parents were not going to stand up for her why should she.

I have no clue as to why I was thinking about that as we crossed the front gates towards the house. Maybe it was because I tried to push people away so they didn't get hurt or was it because I was so used to doing everything on my own. I had no time to think of it now because Royce was coming around to my door and grabbing my hand to lead me inside. He isn't talking and he loves to talk is he waiting for me to start talking? I don't know what to say. Please give me an out and start the conversation, please I begging you. I don't know what to say. I have too much running though my mind. I am silently begging him. I am hoping he gets it because I am clueless on what to concentrate on first. Just when I thought all was lost Royce comes to my rescue.

"Honey, you are never going to have to fight your battles alone. You are now going to have family that wants to help you. I know you had a lonely childhood and thought no one would ever come to your help. You thought people would just use you and mold you into what they wanted.

Well that is not going to happen anymore. I love you and I am going to take care of you."

"Royce, that is all well and good. It would be great if I could just turn off all my thoughts and feelings about having to do everything myself. Trust me, but I don't think you understand the severity of this situation. Do you realize that I didn't speak hardly at all for the first sixteen years of my life?"

"Lexi, from what you told me I knew you spent a lot of time alone."

"Its not that though, when my dad would take me to my skating lessons on Saturday mornings he would ask what was on my mind because he said I looked sad and I needed to smile. I would mutter an easy nothing and stare out the window. There were many opportunities for me to talk but I chose not to speak my mind because I was and still am afraid of how people would see me. My thoughts and dreams were stupid and they are still stupid. That is why I didn't talk and still don't talk much unless its a humor or not important topic. My mind forgets important dates or what not and I don't like people correcting me. It makes me feel dumb and stupid and like I am a baby who needs a bottle and a nap."

There were no words after that. I don't blame him. I just dumped a lot of information at him. I mean how is someone supposed to act after something like that. So I changed the topic.

"Royce I am going to get some cola, then sit out on the porch. I won't leave I promise just go back to work. There is nothing more to talk about."

With that said I walked to the kitchen and then out to sit on the porch swing. Well that was an interesting conversation and I didn't want to get into all of that but apparently I needed to. I am exhausted after all that.

CHAPTER EIGHTY-SEVEN

ROYCE

What is she talking about being mostly mute for the first sixteen years of her life? She never sounds stupid to me, I think she is very informed and has great thoughts. It is time to talk to my brother, I need to take a step back with the everyday duties of the ranch. It is time to put the effort into this relationship.

As I pull my phone out I can't forget everything she just told me. I am mindlessly dialing my brothers number. "Hey did you get back to the ranch yet?"

"Yeah we are just pulling through the front gate. What do you need?"

"I need to just sit and talk and I think Dakota and Lexi could use some girl talk."

"This sounds serious, we will be right there."

"Okay just come into the study and Dakota can stay with Lexi, she is sitting on the porch."

"Alright we just parked see you in two seconds."

I can hear Jaxson talking to Dakota through the screen

door. I didn't want to not be able to see Lexi, but I also wanted to be able to give her the space that she thought she needed. I could tell that conversation that we had before she went outside took it out of her. Who would want to relive all that. I know I wouldn't want to. I can't stop thinking about this, so much so that I am startled when my brother pats me on the back.

"Holy shoot you scared me."

"Sorry, I thought you heard when we were coming up the stairs."

"No, I guess I was out to lunch. I just can't keep what Lexi told me a few minutes ago out of my head."

"What did you she tell you." So I told him the gist of the conversation. I kept seeing his mouth open wider and wider. He couldn't believe it either. Why would no one want to hear some one talk. Her voice isn't that high pitch nasal sounding, where you want to claw your eyes out and use the heavy duty ear plugs.

"So the main reason I wanted to talk to you is because I am wanting to step back a bit on the day to day of the ranch. I know we have the ranch hands and they are more than capable of handling everything, they proved that when we were in Chicago. I just wanted to get your okay and blessing about it. I feel the need to concentrate on Lexi and put her first."

"I get it. I really do. It has been a blessing having Dakota with me. She loves going to the garage with me, we have learned a lot about each other. Yes, the ranch hands can do all the day to day stuff but I don't want them to make any huge decisions. I mean would you still check in on a daily basis to make sure everything that needs to be done gets done?"

"I wouldn't have it any other way. I would check in but I would only spend maybe an hour or two a day. I just don't want Lexi to feel she is trapped here again. I want to take her out and I want the four of us to be able to go out. Plus we need to get all the decisions final for the wedding. The only thing that is for sure is that we are going to do it in Las Vegas."

"Then I support any decision that you make. You would not put any of our lively hood on the line. You are a good business man, and I love you."

"Thanks. It is going to start tomorrow. I am going to call a meeting of the hands and explain the situation in the morning. I think we need to put up a united front. I am thinking we will do it at seven o'clock. Can you make it?"

"Yeah I will be there. Everything will be good. Don't worry about that and just worry about your girl."

"Thanks, I will see you in the morning. Lets go tell our girls and then maybe we can head to the bar later?"

"Oh yeah."

We walked out to our girls and they were just chatting about nothing. I think Lexi was really happy that Dakota came over. She looks a little better. I am still worried about her though. "Hey Lexi and Dakota, we have something we want to share with you."

"What's up Royce?"

"Jaxson and I decided that we are going to step back from the day to day on the ranch a little bit. So we can spend more time with our girls."

"Wait, Dakota goes with Jaxson when he goes to the shop. Your the only one that is really in the day to day with the ranch. What is really going on Royce?"

"Nothing, I just want to spend more time with you. We need to start planning our wedding, I don't want you to be alone all the time."

"And on that note, Dakota, I think it is time we get going. See you guys later, let me know if you still want to go to the bar." Jaxson mentions in between Lexi and I having a little squabble.

"Okay talk to you guys later."

I don't want to fight but this time I think I have to put my foot down. She needs me now more than ever. I am not going to trap her on the ranch, that didn't help us the last time. I think we need to just go on about our lives and not run and hide like last time. One thing is for sure Lexi will not be going anywhere without me.

CHAPTER EIGHTY-EIGHT

LEXI

I don't want him to put his lively hood on hold for me. That is the last thing I want. I don't know what I am going to do about Justin but I know one thing is for sure, he must die or else he will never leave me alone.

So I am putting my foot down. "Royce you can not just stop working the day to day on the farm. I will be okay. Yes I want to spend time with you but I also don't want to take you from your work. That is not how I want our relationship to go."

"Baby girl, I am not stopping work completely. It will be like a long vacation except that the guys will keep me in the loop. We will have like weekly meetings and Jaxson and I will still make all the large decisions. I am just stepping back on the everyday chores and during the weekly meetings we will hash out all the items that needs to be done that week. It will work. I am not trapping you hear on the ranch this time. We are not going to hide. We are going to live our life, plan this wedding and I am not going to be with you every step of the way. We go to all appointments together."

Well that did sound fine. It didn't sound like I was keeping him from anything but I still felt like I was keeping him from important stuff. I don't need him to go with me to doctors appointments, but maybe to pick out a cake flavor would be nice. "Fine we will try it your way, but you don't need to go to doctors appointments and stuff with me. I will be fine."

"Don't think so. You go somewhere I go as well. That is nonnegotiable, if it isn't me then we will have to get you a security detail. In fact I might do that just to be extra careful. You are precious to me. We are not taking any chances got it." He is telling me while he is staring his eyes into me.

"Fine, I guess you win. Let's go get started on all the wedding details. But, first I need to call my sister and tell her the great news."

"Yes, yes you do. I hope she is happy for you. Do you think we should pick out a wedding date before calling. That way we can do travel arrangements as well. I was thinking maybe we could fly to pick her and her possible significant other."

"That would be cool, I can give her that option if you want. But I don't want to wait too long. I want to get married like January Second. We will spend New Years Eve in Vegas and then get married."

Royce leans over and kisses me on the head and tells me he thinks that is a great idea. "Okay I am going to go and give her a call."

I walk back to grab my phone and then get comfortable on the front porch swing.

"Hello?" I hear a hesitant voice.

"McKenna?" Maybe this was a bad idea. I should just hang up on her.

"Yes. This is she."

"It's your sister, Alexus."

"Lexi? Is that really you?"

"Yeah how are you?"

"I am good, how are you doing?"

"I am good, I wanted to call and tell you that I am getting married. I want you to be able to come. We are going to Las Vegas. I am not telling mom and dad because they didn't care about me so why do I care if they see me happy."

"Wow, I would love to be able to come. When is it?"

"We decided on January Second. Oh and Royce, that is my mans name wanted to say that we can come and pick you and if you have a plus one up. Oh my gosh I can't believe I have a man! Sorry I am just so excited and the fact that you still had the same number gives me chills. Can we get to know each other again as adults and maybe become more than sisters, but maybe a friend to each other?"

"Holy cow, Lexi catch your breath." She says giggling. "When would we leave, I am thinking I might be able to go."

"Can I have your email? I will email you all the details because truthfully we just got engaged like two days ago and we only know the date that we want to get married on."

"Sure, my email is java3@hotmail. com."

"Great I will get all the details to you in the next couple of days. I am so happy you answered your phone. I can't wait to see you!"

"Bye Lexi. I will talk to you soon."

I have a huge smile on my face when I walk back in and see Royce sitting on the couch.

"Lets get planning baby, I want to get married!"

"That we can do."

CHAPTER EIGHTY-NINE

JUSTIN

Stupid woman, I should have killed her. That was my first plan anyway before the boyfriend came along. I am supposed to be the boyfriend even if I dumped her. She is not allowed to date anyone else. Doesn't she know that? Well if she thinks I am going to be spending the rest of my life in a cell then she has another thing coming.

I barely spent two days in jail. Money talks and Lexi has no clue that I am not sitting behind bars, because I never went into the system. After the cops "arrested me", my father called and explained that there was a mistake and so I was never charged. I have no idea what was said but all I know is I did not attempt to murder someone. The way my father spun it, I was the guy who was trying to stop it. Man, people can be so stupid. It is good to be me or at least have my family's name.

Little miss prissy Lexi is heading back to Montana with Mr. Money-pants and now it is time to finish what

I started. I am going to kill her, so whatever evidence she has against me will be no longer. The bitch must die and I am going to see to it, and I am going to get away with it. Just. Watch. Me.

You have been invited to see

Alexus Green

marry

Royce James

On January 2nd, 2016 on the outside
observation deck at the Stratosphere
Holet and Casino

The Festiviteies start at 3 O'clock
Dinner Party to follow